He shouldered the door closed behind him

"What do you want?" Abby could read nothing in Lance's face, and it unnerved her.

"This." Stepping into the room, he pulled her roughly into his arms. There was a mastery in his embrace, a hard demanding possessiveness, and Abby's response required no acting ability. Something inside her seemed to ignite and burst into flame.

"I've been wanting to do that since the first moment I saw you," he said, letting her go.

Abby was staring at him wide-eyed and open-mouthed. My God, she thought, did he always kiss like that? No wonder poor Sara Bradbury had fallen for him.

Lance stood back looking at her with a rather rueful smile. "I'm sorry— have I taken you by surprise?"

Books by Sally Wentworth

HARLEQUIN PRESENTS

HARLEQUIN ROMANCES

These books may be available at your local bookseller.

For a free catalog listing all titles currently available, send your name and address to:

Harlequin Reader Service
P.O. Box 52040, Phoenix, AZ 85072-2040
Canadian address: Stratford, Ontario N5A 6W2

SALLY WENTWORTH

backfire

Harlequin Books

TORONTO • NEW YORK • LONDON
AMSTERDAM • PARIS • SYDNEY • HAMBURG
STOCKHOLM • ATHENS • TOKYO • MILAN

Harlequin Presents first edition April 1984
ISBN 0-373-10686-6

Original hardcover edition published in 1983
by Mills & Boon Limited

CHAPTER ONE

As the final curtain came down the audience applauded perfunctorily but politely, and the cast knew that the play was a flop. They had suspected it, of course, right from the first reading, but there was always the faint hope that they could be wrong and they had done their best to put life into a dull script. But if it received only this mediocre reception on the first night at a small new town theatre it wouldn't stand a chance in front of the critical theatregoers in London or any of the big provincial cities that the producers had planned to go on to. As the actors grouped on the stage ready for the first curtain call, they carefully avoided looking into each other's eyes, knowing that the endless search for work would have to start all over again.

The curtain went up and they all bowed, the two principals stepped forward and then it was the turn of the lesser players. As Abigail Stevens came forward for her turn she was gratified to hear the applause pick up a little—from those members of the audience who weren't already putting on their coats and leaving. The curtain came down again and that was it, no more clapping for even a second call, just the shuffling of people leaving their seats and sporadic conversation.

Limply, their carefully built-up egos deflated yet again, the members of the cast headed for their dressing rooms to change into their everyday clothes. Abigail took off the sophisticated black velvet evening dress she had worn for the last act, careful not to get make-up on it; the cast had had to use their own clothes for the play and that dress had cost quite a large part of her salary even though she had got it at a nearly new shop. Looking at her face in the big, well-lit mirror, she felt too down to bother to remove her stage make-up; she'd do it when she got back to her digs, but she unpinned her hair and brushed it out, letting it fall in thick waves the colour of ripe glossy chestnuts down her back.

She shared the dressing-room with two other women: one a middle-aged actress who played the part of the mother in the show, the other a girl younger than herself who was the ingénue. Abigail had been the femme fatale.

'Anybody coming for a drink?' the middle-aged actress queried. 'I could do with one after tonight!'

'Me, too,' Abigail agreed, and glanced at the third girl, Janie, enquiringly. She nodded but didn't speak, and Abby saw that she was close to tears. This had been her first decent part and she had had such high hopes for it, now heavens knew when another chance would come along.

Abby looked at her compassionately and crossed the room to put a friendly hand on her shoulder. 'Come on, let's go and drown our sorrows.'

The theatre was a very modern one, built soon after the new town in the home counties had been established. It had two bars, a restaurant and also a small cinema that showed films that appealed to minor but intellectual audiences. The three women, by tacit consent, made their way to the bar just off the foyer where they found the men in the cast, plus the producer, stage manager and a couple of technicians. Only the leading lady, whose once famous name had been supposed to carry the show, had gone straight home. There was an atmosphere of utter gloom over them all, which no one had the strength or inclination to try to lighten.

'Come join us,' one of the men said to Abby, pulling up a chair for her. 'Let's all wallow in misery together.'

'How long do you think it will run for?' Janie asked them anxiously.

The leading man shrugged. 'If the audiences don't pick up this week then I reckon that will be that. There's no point in taking a flop on to other towns; the backers will probably cut their losses rather than lose any more money.'

'But can't they alter the play? Rewrite it to make it better?'

The producer shook his head regretfully. 'No good, I'm afraid. It's a flop, and we've just got to face up to the fact.'

They went on discussing the bad news, and it was some time before Abby sensed that she was being watched. Glancing round, she saw a man looking at her intently from a table a few yards away. He was a middle-aged man, his hair going grey at the temples, wearing a well-cut dark business suit and a pair of gold-framed glasses. He also looked well off, there was a gold watch on his left wrist and a solid gold ring on the same hand, and he had that scrubbed 'never been dirty' look that only the rich possess. When he saw her looking at him he didn't look away but nodded briefly. Abby wondered if she'd met him, but she had a good memory for faces and decided she hadn't, so she didn't acknowledge him and turned away; she was used to strangers trying to get to know her for her looks or her profession. But two minutes later the barman came over to them and said that the man at the other table had seen the play and would like to buy them all a drink.

'I never turned a free drink down yet,' one man quipped, and took it on himself to accept for all of them. When the drinks came they all dutifully looked over at the stranger and smiled or nodded their thanks.

Ten minutes later, when the glasses were empty, the stage manager stood up. 'Well, I'm for home before the wife locks me out!'

The others watched him go enviously, knowing that he'd have a job next week where they probably wouldn't.

'I think I'll take up stage management or something,' Abby remarked.

'What—with your looks?' the leading man exclaimed. 'You're not serious?'

'Yes, I am. I've been thinking about it for some time.'

'But you can't,' Janie protested. 'You're just starting to make a name for yourself. And you're—you're beautiful!'

Abby smiled at her. 'Thanks, but beautiful girls are two a penny in this profession. And there are always more, younger ones coming along. Such as yourself,' she added, seeing despair in the other girl's eyes. 'No, unless a hit play or a television series comes along soon, I think I'll have had it.'

They broke up soon after that and Abby prepared to leave with Janie and a couple of the others who were staying in the same digs, but as they turned to go, the man at the other table also stood up and came over to her.

'Excuse me, Miss Stevens. I wonder if I might have a word with you before you go.' His voice was well-modulated, a public school accent.

'I'm so sorry,' Abby said, preparing to give him the brush off, 'but we have to catch the last bus.'

'I will of course be happy to pay for a taxi if you could spare me a few minutes of your time. On what is, I assure you, a purely *business* matter,' he emphasised.

'Sorry, but I'm tired and . . .'

'It could perhaps lead to some work for you,' the man said smoothly.

Abby hesitated, wondering if the man were an agent or something, although he didn't look like it. More likely that he had seen her in the play and fancied her. It wasn't the first time it had happened to her by any means, but there was always the chance that he meant what he said, and in her position she couldn't afford to turn down even the sightest chance. She nodded to the others who were waiting by the door. 'I'll see you back at the digs.'

The man pulled a chair out for her and she sat down opposite him. 'Would you like another drink?'

She shook her head. 'Just what is it you want to discuss, Mr . . .?'

'Bradbury. Charles Bradbury.' He took a small silver card case from his pocket, extracted a card and handed it to her. It just gave his name and an address in St John's Wood, one of the most expensive residential areas of London. 'I happened to be here on business today,' he told her, 'and the man I was seeing brought me to lunch in the theatre restaurant. I saw your photograph in the foyer, advertising the play, and I decided to come along and see it.' He hesitated, then said, 'You see,

I've been searching for someone who looks like you for some time.'

'Really? What for?' Abby demanded bluntly, still suspicious.

'The story is rather involved, and before I tell it I would like your assurance that it would go no further. It doesn't only concern me, you see.'

'No, I'm afraid I don't see,' she said impatiently. 'Look, you said this could lead to a part for me.'

'I said it could lead to some work, to some acting work,' Charles Bradbury corrected her. 'And it would be well paid. If you could give me your assurance . . .?'

'Oh, very well,' Abby agreed. 'But I really am tired, Mr Bradbury.'

'Of course. I'll try to be as brief as possible.' Clearing his throat, he went on, 'I'm a business-man, Miss Stevens. The director of several companies in the City under the corporate title of Bradbury Holdings. Naturally I have rivals in my profession, men who envy what I have and who would like to have some of it for themselves. It's the sort of rivalry and cut-and-thrust that goes on in any walk of life where there are ambitious people. Usually it's a friendly rivalry.' He paused, then went on more slowly, 'But eighteen months or so ago one of my companies scooped a large order from under the nose of another. The head of that company didn't like it—not one little bit.' Charles Bradbury's voice grew dry. 'So he decided to get his own back on me in the one area where I was vulnerable—through my daughter.'

'Your daughter?' Abby echoed in surprise, interested in his story despite herself, his world of big business completely alien to her.

'Yes.' He took a clean handkerchief from his

pocket, took off his glasses and began to polish them. His eyes looked strangely older and more vulnerable without the hardness of the glass. 'My daughter was very young, very susceptible. This man . . .' He seemed to find the words difficult to say. 'This man took her young life and ruined it— ruined it completely.'

'How?' Abby asked gently after a moment when he didn't seem able to go on.

He hesitated. 'I really would rather not go into that, if you don't mind. Suffice it to say that ever since, I've been looking for a way to bring this man down, and now I think I have it. I've heard the merest whisper that he may be acting illegally in the way he's using his company monies. It's rather technical to explain to someone who isn't conversant with the stock market,' he added, guessing correctly that Abby knew nothing about it at all.

'Well, I can understand that you want to be revenged on this man, but I really can't see where I could possibly come into it,' said Abby in puzzlement.

Charles Bradbury started to speak, but the barman came over and interrupted him. 'I'm sorry, but it's eleven o'clock and I have to close the bar.'

'I don't want any more drinks, but I would like to finish my conversation with this lady.' He took a large denomination note from his wallet and passed it to the barman. 'Perhaps you could go and smoke a cigarette or something for half an hour. Oh, and could you please order a taxi for eleven-thirty?'

The barman looked at the note and his eyes widened. 'Yes, of course, sir. I'll do it right away.'

Abby watched him go, only mildly surprised at his sudden obsequiousness; money had that effect on people. She realised that Bradbury was watching her and she turned back to him, wondering just what had happened to his daughter to make him want revenge so badly, because even though he covered it well there was hatred in his voice when he spoke of his rival.

He cleared his throat again; a nervous habit he seemed to have. 'As I was saying, there might just be a chance that this man is acting illegally. It might not be true, of course, it might just be a rumour that someone who has reason to dislike him has put round. But the only way to find out, one way or another, is to get close to him, to find out his secrets. And that, Miss Stevens, is where I thought you might come in.'

Abby stared at him. 'You mean you want me to try and get close to a man who's already ruined your daughter?' She got angrily to her feet. 'You must be mad to think that I'd even contemplate such a thing! And for your information, I'm not the kind of girl who would—get close to a man, as you put it—for money!'

She turned to march out of the bar, but Bradbury, too, had got to his feet and caught her arm. 'Good. I'm glad to hear it.' She looked at him in surprise and he said quickly, 'Please don't misunderstand me, Miss Stevens. I don't want you to get as close as—er—you suggest to La ...' he stopped himself in time from saying his enemy's name, 'to this man. I wouldn't dream of asking such a thing. No, I just want you to become friendly with him. You're an actress; I'm sure you're quite capable of holding a man at arm's length if you want to.'

'Possibly,' Abby admitted. 'But why me?'

'Because you're the type he goes for. I found out that he was once engaged and I obtained a photograph of his ex-fiancée. You could be her double.'

'But why ex-fiancée? If they broke it off it would probably have put him off anyone who looked like her,' Abby pointed out rather tartly. Surely Bradbury had realised such an obvious point.

'Ah, but it wasn't broken off. The girl was killed in a car accident only a few weeks before the wedding.'

Abby sat back in her chair, thinking about it. 'And he hasn't married or become engaged since?'

'No.'

'How old is he?'

'Thirty-four.'

'And when was his fiancée killed?'

'Almost seven years ago. He's had girl-friends since, of course, plenty of them, from the reports I've gathered, but none of them have lasted very long and there has never been any hint that he was contemplating marriage with any of them.'

'These girl-friends,' Abby said. 'Did any of them look like his fiancée?'

Bradbury shook his head. 'From what I've been able to gather—and I've been quite thorough— none of them looked even remotely like her.'

Abby looked at him contemplatively. Yes, he would have been thorough. She could imagine him systematically setting out to gather every little piece of information about his enemy so that he could eventually destroy him as his daughter had been destroyed. Calmly, without any outward show of emotion, like a spider with a fly, gradually drawing nearer and nearer to his prey. Abby shivered, glad that she wasn't the fly. She shook her head in sudden decision. 'No, I'm sorry, Mr Bradbury, but I really don't want to get mixed up in this. You'll have to find someone else.'

'I can appreciate your feeling that way, Miss Stevens,' Charles Bradbury told her, in no way put out. 'But—forgive me for being frank—although you played your part well, that play isn't good enough to run for very long, and it certainly isn't good enough to get into the West End. I'm not familiar with the employment situation in—er—show business and I don't know what future prospects you have, but I should have thought the offer of short term and extremely well paid work worth a little more consideration than being turned down out of hand,' he pointed out mildly.

'Yours is hardly a normal offer of work,' Abby retorted.

'Which is why it is extremely well paid. And although, as I've said, I'm not familiar with show business myself, I have a great many business contacts who are, and I would make sure, after you have completed your task for me, that they knew that it would oblige me if they considered your name for any suitable parts that came along. I would, in fact, use all my not inconsiderable influence to further your career.'

Which could mean anything, Abby thought, looking at him, depending entirely on just how much influence he really had; he might think he had far more than he actually did.

'You say short term?' she asked cautiously.

'Yes. I couldn't give you a definite time limit, I'm afraid. It would depend entirely on how quickly you became on friendly terms with this man. But I'm sure it couldn't take more than three months at the very outside. And there's always the possibility, of course, that he might not be drawn to you at all. He might just ignore you.'

Abby smiled slightly to herself at that; she wasn't in the habit of being ignored, especially when she put herself out to captivate a man.

'As to your fee,' Bradbury went on, 'whether or not this man is drawn to you, I will pay you one thousand pounds for the—er—attempt. Should he show signs of wanting to get to know you better, I will give you another thousand pounds for you to spend on clothes so that you can dress the part, and those you may keep. I will also rent a flat for you in a fashionable part of London until our object is completed, at which time I will give you a further payment of another four thousand pounds. Any extra expensive accessories you need, such as furs and jewels, I will hire for you, and I will of course pay any out-of-pocket expenses.'

Abby's mouth came open at the beginning of this speech and stayed open until the end. She gulped. 'You must want your revenge on this man extremely badly!'

'I do,' Bradbury said gravely, taking off his glasses and wiping them again. 'And luckily I'm an extremely rich man, because I don't care how much it costs me to get it.'

She looked at him, trying to weigh him up. He didn't look particularly ruthless, quite mild-mannered really, but you could never tell with that well-bred, self-effacing type. But if he ran a large company he must have trodden on a few toes to get there. Or perhaps it was only what had happened to his daughter that had made him ruthless. On impulse she asked, 'Just what did he do to your daughter, Mr Bradbury? I think I have the right to know that before I come to a decision. And you keep calling him "that man". Who is he?'

'I've been careful to avoid using his name until you knew the full story and had made up your mind. And as for my daughter ...' His face twisted, 'I agree that you have the right to ask, but I would rather not go into that until you've agreed the idea in principle.'

Abby looked at him for a long moment, then stood up. 'In that case, Mr Bradbury, I must refuse your offer. You're asking me to take too much on trust. You've asked me to get close to a man who could be dangerous, and although you've said I needn't become closer than a friend, the man might not be willing to stop at that. You've refused to tell me who he is or what he's done to your daughter. And you haven't said exactly what it is you want me to do if I do get close to him. No, I'm sorry. I don't want to take it on.' He didn't say anything and she added rather defensively, 'For all you know I could be married or something and not free to take on something like this.'

'But you're not,' he answered calmly. 'After I saw your photograph at lunchtime I made some enquiries about you, and I know that you're quite free. I wouldn't have asked you otherwise.'

Abby stared at him, wondering where he had got the information. From her agent, presumably. And if he knew that then he must also know that she had no acting prospects at all, only long weeks of living on the dole and haunting all the casting agencies in the hope of landing an audition. But she still shook her head obstinately. 'No—I'm sorry. You'll have to find someone else.'

He didn't seem at all angry or put out. 'Will you

please keep my card and think about it? I hope that you'll change your mind. And I must, of course, ask you to treat what I've told you in the strictest confidence for my daughter's sake.' He got to his feet. 'In the meantime I'm sure your taxi must be here.' He took a fiver from his wallet and passed it to her. 'Will this cover the fare?'

Abby didn't want to take the money, but he insisted, saying that he had made her miss her bus and he had promised her a taxi home. In the end she took the money because it was easier than saying no. He escorted her out of the theatre and saw her into the cab. 'Please don't hesitate to phone me if you change your mind or would like to discuss it further,' he told her as he held the door for her.

As Abby tiptoed to her room a little later, afraid of waking the other boarders, she was quite sure that she wouldn't change her mind, nevertheless she couldn't put it out of her head, it kept churning round and round in her brain, keeping her awake far into the night. She could sympathise with Charles Bradbury in some ways, but she really didn't see why she should allow herself to be used to get his revenge on this man, whoever he was. Especially as he wouldn't even take her entirely into his confidence. But Abby was only human, and when she thought of all that lovely money, and the clothes a thousand pounds would buy, she did give a groan of disappointment. If she couldn't find work, five thousand pounds would have been enough to keep her for two years, three if she was really careful. It would have meant that she could have spent all her time looking for work instead of taking part-time jobs to try and make ends meet, with the possibility of missing the one chance that

might have made all the difference. She sighed and
turned over in the uncomfortable bed, trying to
push it out of her mind, but it was a long time
before she at last drifted off to sleep.

The backers valiantly kept the play running for
another week and the cast travelled to Bristol to
stage it, but here again they met with the same
cool reception and no one felt any surprise when
the producer told them that it was being
abandoned. On the Sunday morning Abby
travelled back to London by train with most of the
rest of the cast. Strangely enough it wasn't a
gloomy journey. Actors are naturally optimistic
people; they have to be or they would go mad. Most
of them went on believing that the big break was
just around the corner, and it sometimes took
nearly their whole lifetime before many of them
could see that there just weren't any more corners
to go round. So they talked and joked, exchanged
experiences and played cards, and shared the
bottles of plonk they'd bought to drink with their
British Rail sandwiches. By the end of the journey
they had all exchanged telephone numbers and
promises to let each other know if they heard of
anything suitable coming up.

Abby lived in a flat just off Clapham Common
which she shared with three other girls, all
actresses. There were only two bedrooms, but as
one or other of them was usually on the road or
off on location somewhere, it wasn't too over-
crowded. And anyway, the only way they could
afford the rent and expenses was by sharing it
among the four of them. Abby took the
Underground and then a bus and got home in the
middle of the afternoon. None of the others were
in, so she was able to have a leisurely bath and

wash her hair. As she dried herself she looked at her pale skin and wished she could afford a course on a sun-bed; you always looked so much healthier and more vital when you were brown. Well, she'd just have to wait until the summer, which was still a few months away, and try to get a tan naturally.

The girl that Abby shared a room with was away that weekend and the other two, Sue and Liz, didn't come home until about ten-thirty, when Abby was sitting in her housecoat in front of the electric fire, drinking cocoa and watching television.

'Hi,' Sue greeted her. 'What are you doing back?'

'It folded,' Abby answered laconically.

'Oh, no!' They dropped down on to the floor beside her and she told them about it as they listened sympathetically. They were both working at the moment so could afford to be generous with their comfort and reassurance.

'What are you going to do now?' Liz asked.

Abby shrugged. 'Go and see Tolly tomorrow, I suppose.' Tolly was John Tollman, her agent.

'You haven't got any auditions or anything lined up?'

She shook her head; she had pushed Charles Bradbury's offer so far to the back of her mind that she didn't even mention it.

'Hey! Wait a minute.' Sue suddenly snapped her fingers. 'They're holding auditions for the part in that new television series tomorrow morning. You know, the one we heard about where the female lead had to drop out at the last minute because she had to go into hospital.'

'That's right,' Liz agreed excitedly. 'We didn't

take too much notice because they wanted someone who could start straight away, and we were both under contract. Now where was it?' She frowned, trying to remember.

'What sort of series?' Abby wanted to know.

'Comedy. It's for six episodes to start with; more if it takes. And it's supposed to be a honey of a part. Who was it told us about it, Liz?'

'I'm trying to think.' Her frown grew deeper. 'Ah, I know! It was that girl I worked with in pantomime last year. You remember, Abby—Carol something. She thought we might be interested, although she wasn't going herself. Now where's her number?' Liz opened their precious telephone index which was crammed with numbers of other actors and contacts, any one of which might some day be useful. 'Yes, here it is—Carol Kaye. I'd better phone her right away or she'll be in bed.'

The phone call lasted only a few minutes and then Liz put down the receiver, the piece of paper she'd made notes on in her hand. 'Yes, we were right; the audition's tomorrow morning at ten-thirty at the Wood Green Studios. The producer is Paul Tait and the series is called "Better the Devil You Know". Sounds as if it could be quite good.'

'Thanks,' Abby said gratefully. 'At least it's a chance.'

But when Abby got to the Studios the next morning it seemed that half the actresses in London also wanted the chance. The place was crowded and she almost had to fight her way in.

'Name, please.' A harassed man at the door was preparing a list. Abby gave her name and he pushed a printed paper into her hand. 'Fill this in, would you?' It was a form asking her to list her qualifications, experience and previous television appearances. Abby found a pen and had to use her bag to rest on while she filled in the form as best she could; she clipped a photo of herself to it and then struggled back to the door to hand it in and settled down to wait. There were several girls she knew there and, although they were all on tenterhooks about the audition and longing to get the part, there was very little acrimony; they had all been through the same scene too many times for that. After about an hour someone came into the crowded room where they were waiting, announced that the following people wouldn't be called for an audition and read out a list of names. Abby gave a long sigh of relief when hers wasn't on it. Not that that meant too much; there was still a long way to go. It was well into the afternoon before her name was called. There were several people watching the auditions, all of them looking rather jaded and with lots of plastic cups that had contained coffee on the tables in front of them. The only one Abby recognised was Paul Tait; his thick hair, so fair that it was almost white, made him recognisable anywhere.

Abby was introduced to the actor who was to feed her her lines. She had been given a couple of pages of script to study earlier, and the wait had been so long that she had learnt the lines by heart, which was a great help as she could concentrate on putting them over without having to continually refer to the script. It must also have impressed the producer, because she was heard all the way through, whereas some of the girls who had gone before her had come out very quickly. Afterwards they talked among themselves for several minutes, then Paul Tait, running a harassed hand through his hair, asked her several questions about her past experience. 'Okay,' he said at last. 'Hang around, will you?'

Filled with hope, Abby bought herself a cup of coffee from the vending machine and settled down to wait again. When she wasn't actually acting, most of her time seemed to be spent sitting around and waiting. She had brought a book with her, but was so on edge that she couldn't settle to read it. Was it her imagination, or did they seem to be getting through the rest of the waiting girls more quickly now? At six-thirty they called her in to read the part again, then Paul Tait told her she'd got the job. 'But only if you can start immediately,' he warned her.

'Oh, I can. I was supposed to be in work for at least the next two months, but it fell through.'

'Fine. Have you got an agent?'

'Yes. John Tollman.'

He nodded, running an impatient hand through his hair again. 'I know. Okay, I'll have the contract made out and get in touch with him tomorrow so that, with any luck, you'll be able to start work on Wednesday or Thursday. Come and meet the others.'

He introduced her to the people sitting with him to watch the auditions, all of them relaxed and friendly now that they had reached a decision. Abby received their congratulations with her head in a whirl. At last! The break she'd waited for so long. And to think she'd been sorry that wretched play had folded! Paul Tait gave her the script for the first episode in the series to take home and study, and she diligently read it all through the long journey home on the tube, but was so excited that she hardly took it in. Liz and Sue were equally excited when they heard, and that night they celebrated with a meal in their local Chinese restaurant, gorging themselves on spare ribs and sweet and sour.

As early as she could the following morning, Abby telephoned Tolly and told him the good news. 'Great,' he answered. 'It looks as if you're on the way up. Better come into the office about four this afternoon to sign the contract. We should have it all settled by then.'

The rest of the day passed blissfully as Abby caught up with her washing and ironing, cleaned up the flat and did the shopping. At four she was shown into Tolly's office, smiling happily.

He looked up at her and quickly away, his expression a far cry from the wide grin she'd expected.

'Sit down, Abby. I'm afraid I've got bad news.'

'Oh, no!' She stared at him, already knowing what was coming.

'They changed their minds,' he told her. 'I put up a fight for you, but nothing had been signed, so there was nothing I could do.'

'But—but why?' Abby exclaimed in distress. 'They *promised* me the part, Tolly! They even gave me a script.'

'They said they'd found someone with more television experience.' Tolly took a cigarette from his pocket and lit it. 'I'm really sorry, girl,' he said again.

Abby looked at him, surprised by the genuine sympathy in his voice; usually he was stoical about that sort of thing. He didn't look at her, just fiddled with some papers on his desk. 'You got anything else lined up?'

She shook her head. 'No. Have you?'

'They're looking for some girls for a porno picture.'

'You say that every time I come in here,' Abby pointed out exasperatedly. 'Haven't you got any real work for me?'

He shook his head. 'You know what the business is like. I'll ring you if anything comes up. Sorry girl,' he repeated.

Abby was so disappointed she could have cried. But there was nothing she could do. As Tolly said, it had only been a verbal promise. She was back where she started, all her bright hopes turned to disillusion.

Bad luck seemed to dog her footsteps; twice more in the next month the chance of work came along only to be lost, once because somehow the instructions from Tolly had got muddled and she'd arrived for an audition on the wrong day, and the second because the contract for her to play a small part in a one-off dramatised documentary got lost in the post. Abby was almost in despair, her money had run out and everything seemed to be going wrong. She would just have to try and get another part time job to tide her over until some real work came along. But even the Job Centre had nothing for her; usually a good-looking girl could get short term work doing market research or store demonstrations, but there was just nothing doing, so she had to sign on the dole again.

However, the following day the bell at the flat rang and when Liz went to answer it she found a uniformed chauffeur outside with a note for Abby. 'Perhaps it's some television work,' she said hopefully, passing over the note.

Abby opened it quickly, all sorts of wild fantasies going through her brain. To her disappointment the note was from Charles

Bradbury, the man who had made her that crazy proposition. It said: 'Dear Miss Stevens, I wonder if you have given any further thought to the offer I made you? Should you still be undecided I am now able to answer any questions you might have. I should also like you to meet my daughter. Perhaps we could have lunch together today. The chauffeur will wait as long as necessary and bring you to meet me.'

'What is it?' Liz demanded. 'Is it work?'

'Sort of,' Abby admitted. 'A man who saw me in the play thought I'd be right for a project he's got in mind.'

'What sort of part? How long a run?'

'I—I'm not sure. Could be for three months, but it might be just a few days.'

'Will you take it?'

Abby shrugged. 'It's not a regular sort of part. And I'd have to live—er—nearer the job if it was successful.'

Liz, ever practical, asked. 'How much is he offering?'

'A thousand pounds, whether or not it lasts, and five if it does.'

'And you're thinking twice about it? Abby Stevens, you must be mad! Nobody turns down that kind of money.' Liz stared at her. 'Unless—he doesn't want you to sleep with him, does he?'

'No, nothing like that. But it's—out of the ordinary.'

'So tell me.'

'I can't; I promised him I wouldn't.'

Liz took the note from her and read it. 'Are you going?'

Abby sighed. 'I don't know. I don't want to, but nothing's going right lately.'

'Well, you don't have to accept his offer even if you do go. And at least you'll get a free lunch out of it.'

'There is that,' Abby laughed. She came to a sudden decision. 'Okay, tell the chauffeur to pick me up in half an hour.'

Thirty minutes later exactly he rang the bell again and the chauffeur showed Abby into a big black Mercedes. She expected him to take her to one of the more sedate London restaurants like the Savoy Grill, but instead the grey-uniformed driver picked up the South Circular Road and was soon heading out of London to the expensive commuter belt area of Surrey. Perhaps their lunch, then, was to be at Charles Bradbury's home. That, of course, was far more likely if his daughter was to be there. But it seemed that she was wrong, because the car stopped momentarily at the entrance to a gated driveway that had a discreet bronze plate saying 'The Cassell Clinic' on the wall. The gates opened electronically and they swept up a very long gravelled driveway to a large brick mansion— except that most mansions didn't have bars at all the upper windows.

The chauffeur led her into the house and across to a pleasant room near the entrance where Charles Bradbury was waiting for her.

'Ah, Miss Stevens. How nice to see you again. I'm so glad that you were able to come.'

Abby returned his greeting, aware that his eyes were carefully going over her elegant black suit and the chic little hat with the half veil that she'd got for half price after they were provided for a television part. He nodded approvingly. 'Have you thought about my offer, Miss Stevens?'

'No, I haven't,' she replied honestly. 'I'd

almost forgotten about it until your note came today.'

'I see. Well, perhaps now we could go and see my daughter. This way.' He led her outside into the entrance hall and then motioned her to wait while he went over to the reception desk and spoke to the woman on duty there. She rang a bell and within seconds a uniformed nurse came and led them upstairs and down a long corridor with doors opening off it that all had those little trapdoors in that could be slid back so that you could see the person inside.

They came to a room at the end and the nurse looked through the trapdoor, then she selected a key from a bunch that jangled on a chain hung from her belt and unlocked the door.

Abby hadn't known what to expect; she had a vivid imagination and during that walk along the corridor she had envisaged all kinds of things, progressively terrible, but she had never imagined the pathetically thin girl who lay on a settee, gazing blankly up at the ceiling. It was a large room, with windows on two sides that let in the sunlight—sunlight with black zebra stripes where the metal bars cast a shadow. There wasn't much furniture, just a comfortable-looking bed, the settee and one or two other pieces. No mirror or anything that could possibly be used to do anyone harm. But there were flowers in the room, books, magazines and a television set built into the wall.

After one glance round the room, Abby gave her full attention to the girl on the couch. She looked incredibly young, but that could be because of her thinness and the white pallor of her face. She must have been pretty once, perhaps might even have been beautiful when she had reached

maturity, but she would never be beautiful now,
her skin was mottled and there were scars on her
cheek as if someone had sliced his initials into her
flesh. She didn't look at them as they came in, her
eyes staying fixed on the ceiling, but her hands
plucked incessantly at the blanket that covered her
knees, exactly in the way that the very old seem to
continually touch something for the reassurance
that they are still alive. Reluctantly Abby moved
nearer to the settee when Charles Bradbury put an
elbow under her arm and led her forward. The
nurse stayed discreetly by the door.

'What's the matter with her?' Abby whispered,
although it was obvious that the girl was
completely unaware of them.

'Drugs,' Bradbury replied shortly.

Abby looked at him in horror. 'You mean *he*
gave her drugs?'

His hand tightened on her arm warningly. 'I'll
tell you outside.'

'Can nothing be done for her? Has she come
here to be cured?'

He shook his head. 'She can't be cured. Her
brain has been affected. She will stay like this till
she dies.' He stared down at his daughter silently
for several minutes, then roused himself. 'We
might as well go. Nothing is going to change.'

It was a relief to get outside that sad building
and into the sunlight again.

'Let's stroll in the garden for a while, shall we?'
Bradbury suggested. They walked across the
beautifully-tended lawn and he said, 'I blame
myself. I should have realised what was happening.
But she was seventeen and wanted some freedom.
I was afraid of holding her too close, of not letting
her have any life of her own. And then I was

always so busy, there was always so much work to do.' He gave a bitter laugh. 'The old story, I suppose.'

'Your wife?' Abby suggested gently.

'She died of cancer ten years ago.'

'I'm sorry.'

He nodded, accepting her sympathy. 'And when he got hold of Sarah, my daughter, he— manipulated her so skilfully, turning her against me, making her promise not to tell me because he said I wouldn't have approved. By the time I found out it was too late; she was already hooked on drugs. When I put her in a centre for treatment she ran away. She wasn't found until nearly two months later, lying in the gutter in the state she's in now. God alone knows where she'd been or who with. She must have been treated very cruelly. Her mind was gone when they found her. I've been able to keep her alive, but she's entirely reliant on drugs. Maybe,' he added grimly, 'it would be better if I let her die.'

Abby looked at him, studying his face. Only his voice and the thinness of his mouth betrayed the depth of his emotion. She didn't express an opinion. Who could? Instead she said, 'Who *is* this man?'

Bradbury looked at her quickly, then took his wallet from his pocket and extracted a photograph. 'His name is Lance Lazenby,' he said as he handed it to her. It showed the head and shoulders of a man of about thirty-five looking slightly across to his right. Not a posed study; the subject was obviously quite unaware that he was being photographed. Abby's first impression was that it was a very handsome face, the features clean-cut and fine-boned, then she saw a confused mixture of arrogance in the way he held his head, of strength in the thrust of his jaw, and cynicism in the lines around his mouth. The photo was in black and white so she could only see that his thick hair was dark and slightly longer than average. She guessed he must be tall because his shoulders were so wide; they would have been out of proportion if he was short. Reluctantly she looked at his eyes; for some reason she had been avoiding looking at them. Even in this snapshot there was a hard, ruthless quality in them, a coldness that sent a sudden chill down her spine. And yet Abby could understand why Sarah Bradbury had fallen for him; he was the type who could twist an innocent girl like her around his little finger. Abby looked at his eyes again—and he was the type who would care nothing about destroying her either.

'Did he actually give her the drugs?' Abby asked.

'No. As I said, he only introduced her to them. But you wouldn't have to be afraid,' he assured her. 'He has no reason to connect you with me, and you're forewarned. And far more experienced than my daughter was.'

'I could pull out if there was any danger?' Abby asked quickly.

'Of course. I should insist on it.'

'What exactly would you want me to do?'

Bradbury looked at her intently. 'You mean you'll take it on?'

Abby thought of the girl lying back there in the nursing home, more dead than alive, and then looked again at the snapshot in her hand. 'Yes,' she agreed slowly, 'I rather think I will.'

CHAPTER TWO

LESS than forty-eight hours later Abby was looking at the original of the photograph. From the moment that she had said she would take the job on Charles Bradbury had taken over and things had moved extremely quickly. He had taken her straightaway to the flat in Chelsea that he proposed to rent for her, and Abby had gasped at its size and elegance. It was in the most fashionable part of the borough in a tree-lined street, had a kitchen, sitting-room and study as well as a bedroom and luxury bathroom, and was furnished in a happy mixture of modern comfort and antique perfection. It was the sort of place Abby could only ever have afforded if she had won the lead in a long-running television series, or had become the mistress of an extremely rich man. At the flat, Charles Bradbury had sat her down and given her a brief outline of what he wanted her to do: simply, it was to get close enough to the Lazenby man to plant some sort of bugging device on him, and of course to keep her eyes and ears open for any pieces of information he might drop about his business interests.

'But isn't that against the law—industrial espionage?' Abby had demanded.

'Good heavens, no!' Bradbury looked affronted. 'If I'd asked you to break into his office or something, of course it would be, but to just give Lazenby a present of a pen that happens to have a bug in it can hardly be illegal, now can it?'

'No, I suppose not,' Abby agreed, reassured by his positiveness. 'How would I go about meeting him?'

'I have several ideas on that.' He went on to outline them, but to Abigail they all sounded too contrived, too over-dramatic.

She shook her head. 'It should be a casual meeting, purely by chance.' She thought for a moment, then said, 'Look, if I'm going to play this part I really ought to study it. Can you let me have as much information as possible about him? His interests and hobbies, that kind of thing. And first I'd like to see him without him seeing me. Can you arrange that, do you think?'

'Quite easily. He's addressing a meeting of the shareholders of one of his companies the day after tomorrow. I can get you a pass to go to that. But how will you avoid him seeing you?'

'Don't worry,' Abby assured him, 'I'll be just one of the crowd.'

Which was how she came to be sitting in the sixth row of a shareholders meeting in the conference room of a London hotel, looking up at the raised platform on which the man she was going to try and dupe was sitting in an attitude of relaxed inattentiveness that didn't quite disguise the fact that he was watching the audience's reaction like a hawk. Abby didn't understand much of what was going on herself, but it was evident that the board wanted to introduce some measures that the shareholders weren't too happy about. Somebody at the back got up to protest and there was a general murmur of agreement. The Company Secretary, who was speaking, tried to appease them and make his proposals sound reasonable, but the sounds of dissatisfaction increased and became heated. Lance Lazenby continued to watch for a few minutes, then got lazily to his feet. 'If I might say a few words,' he interrupted easily.

The Secretary gave him a relieved glance and gratefully sat down.

Lazenby began to speak in a deep, well-articulated voice that carried easily to the back of the large room. Abby concentrated on the man and not what he said, which she didn't understand anyway, but she was aware of the gradual change in the audience and realised that he was an experienced and eloquent orator. He had the voice for it, it was rich and reassuring, with the carrying power of an actor's; the sort of voice you could happily go on listening to for hours. But Abby firmly closed her ears and let her eyes take over. She had been right about his being tall; he must be at least six foot three, his height accentuated by the severe dark business suit he was wearing, the handkerchief just showing in his top pocket matching the deep red silk of his tie. The photo had shown just his head and shoulders, but now she could see that his hands were narrow and strong, the long fingers devoid of rings. He had a tan, too, which hadn't shown in the photograph, as if he'd just returned from a hot country.

In her mind, Abby went through the list of Lance Lazenby's interests that Mr Bradbury had given her: racing cars and horses, collecting antique silver, the opera, sailing and skiing. And he belonged to several gaming clubs. He seemed to go in for a lot of sport, and Abby could well believe it; his figure looked fit and athletic under the well-cut suit. And he was certainly rich enough by all accounts to be able to afford the gaming clubs and all that they entailed.

A ripple of applause broke out around her and she switched back on to her surroundings. Evidently his speech had won the majority of the shareholders over, so presumably he had charm as well. A formidable adversary. He was smiling now as the Company Secretary thanked him, but it was a smile that didn't reach his eyes. They took a vote which was passed and the meeting started to break up. Abby left among the first small crowd to go and was on a bus going back to Clapham before she took off the woolly hat she had used to cover her hair and the heavy-rimmed glasses she had worn to help disguise herself. Not that you could call it a disguise really; they were just props she'd used to make herself nondescript, to blend in with the crowd.

Somehow Mr Bradbury had got hold of Lance Lazenby's agenda for the next few days and, after studying it, Abby phoned Bradbury that evening.

'I think my best chance of meeting him casually is at the silver auction at Sotheby's on Friday. Could you get hold of a catalogue for me? I thought I might pretend to collect antique jewellery.'

Bradbury liked the idea and after some discussion he rang off, promising to send the catalogue the next day. He was even better than his word; early the following morning his chauffeur arrived to collect Abby and her luggage and take her to the Chelsea flat, where she found waiting for her not only the catalogue but several books on antique jewellery. And on top of this there was a cheque for two thousand pounds together with introduction cards to firms specialising in the hire of jewellery and furs.

Abby looked at the cheque for several minutes,

holding it reverently; she had never in her life earned such a large amount in one go before. But half of this, she remembered, was for clothes for the part she was to play, and she would stick scrupulously to spending it on that. Judiciously spent, even in these days, a thousand pounds could go quite a long way to collecting a decent wardrobe of clothes. And she did have some quite good things of her own which she could use; she had always tried to buy the best that she could afford rather than the latest fashions, mainly because she never knew when she might have to use her own clothes in a play. She looked forward eagerly to going shopping, but first she had promised herself a real treat: the bathroom in the flat was the most luxurious she had ever seen, done out with a bright red bath and fittings, gold taps, black mirrors on the walls and ceilings and long-pile black carpet on the floor. Abby poured half a bottle of scented oil into the hot water and, positively drooling with sybaritic pleasure, lay back in the bubbles, staying there for ages without the threat of someone banging on the door to tell her to hurry up, as she studied the books on antique jewellery.

On Friday the sun was shining as Abby's taxi pulled up outside the auction rooms. For a few moments she felt the butterflies in her tummy that she always got just before walking on to a stage, but when the uniformed doorman came to hold open the taxi door for her, it was like the curtains opening, and her nerves quietened. Taking a deep breath, she stepped out of the taxi and into the role she was about to play.

She was dressed in a stunning outfit entirely in black and white; black silk blouse with a deep ruffled neck under a severe white wool suit, very high black patent shoes, with matching bag and gloves, and a black hat with a small brim and veil that entirely covered her hair. And round her neck and on her wrist she wore jewellery made of black jet, delicately carved. The whole effect was eye-catching, to say the least, and achieved the look she wanted, elegantly simple but extremely expensive. The doorman rushed to open the door into the auction house for her and Abby calmly made her way into the room where the antique silver was on display, every head turning to look at her as she passed. That Lance Lazenby was already here, she knew; Charles Bradbury had been sitting in his car watching the entrance and had used his car telephone to let her know when to take the short taxi ride.

In the doorway leading to the silver room, Abby paused and looked around. There were already quite a few people there, examining the silver, but she could only see the tops of heads and hear the murmur of voices because of the many glass display cabinets that filled most of the floor space. But she had an actor's ear and once having heard a voice could pick it up again unerringly. Lance Lazenby's deep tones, even though spoken at an ordinary conversational level, carried to her quite clearly, and she crossed the room and began to work her way back towards him so that they would meet somewhere in the middle. After a few minutes a young official came over to her and asked her if she was interested in anything special. Abby gave him a wonderful smile that made him hers for as long as she needed him, and confided her interest in antique jewellery. He was immediately all eager assistance and began pointing

out items in the various cabinets. They came to
one that contained a wide silver bracelet, heavily
chased, and with a clasp in the form of two
swords.

'How unusual,' Abby exclaimed. 'May I see it
more closely?'

The official obligingly unlocked the cabinet and
removed the bracelet from the sweep of blue velvet
on which it lay. Out of the corner of her eyes,
Abby saw that Lance Lazenby was standing only a
couple of yards away, examining a tall silver
chalice, and talking to an older man who was
presumably another official of the auction house.

'What date is it?' Abby asked as she took the
bracelet, raising her voice to a slightly higher pitch.

'Late fifteenth century. It's Italian and reputed
to have been made for Lucrezia Borgia.'

'It's very beautiful.' She allowed a note of doubt
into her voice. 'Are you sure of its authenticity?
I'm sure I've seen something very similar to this
that was a Victorian reproduction.'

It worked like a charm. When she still looked
doubtful after he'd tried to reassure her, the
official turned to his older colleague who was with
Lance Lazenby and asked him to verify it. Abby
turned casually with him and found herself
looking into the cool grey eyes of the man she had
come to find. Without even blinking, she let her
gaze move on to the other man, who had
murmured a word of apology to Lazenby and
moved forward to take the bracelet from her.

'Oh, yes, it's definitely fifteenth century. You
can tell by the way these griffins are chased into
the raised metalwork.' He pointed out some other
details and then turned. 'Don't you agree with me,
Lazenby?' He passed the bracelet on and

explained to Abby, 'Mr Lazenby here is an expert on antique silver.'

Lance Lazenby looked at the bracelet and then handed it back. 'Yes, it's quite genuine. Are you interested in buying it?' he asked, addressing Abby directly.

She experienced a little thrill of triumph that she was careful not to show. 'I think so. I should be even more interested if it could be proved that it had really been made for Lucrezia Borgia.'

'Ah, I'm afraid that we can't guarantee,' the older official said regretfully, as he put the bracelet back in the cabinet.

'What a shame,' Abby remarked regretfully.

'But it could be amusing to try to prove that it was,' Lazenby pointed out.

She allowed her eyes to light with interest and she smiled as she agreed, 'Why, yes, so it could.'

His eyes lingered on her face, but Abby turned away, moving towards the next cabinet. She felt more than saw Lazenby lift a hand, and the two officials who had been about to follow them melted away.

'You're interested in antique jewellery, Miss . . .?'

'Stevens,' Abby supplied. 'Yes, as I was telling your colleague, I collect jewellery that has an interesting history. Not necessarily silver, though.' She held out her wrist. 'This jet jewellery I'm wearing, for instance, was made for Queen Victoria after the death of Prince Albert.'

His hand came up to cup her wrist as he looked at the bracelets, then his eyes travelled slowly up her figure to the jet collar around her neck. 'They're very fine pieces,' he remarked.

Abby's heart started to beat a little faster and

she quickly drew her hand away. 'Are you also an expert on Whitby jet, Mr ... I'm afraid I've forgotten your name,' she said coldly.

'Lazenby,' he supplied, his mouth twisting into a small smile. 'Lance Lazenby. And I'm afraid you've got it wrong: I don't work here, I'm only a customer.'

'Oh, but I thought ...' Sounding disconcerted, Abby said, 'I beg your pardon—I thought you were one of the auctioneers.'

'A natural mistake. But you were telling me about your collection.'

As Abby's 'collection' consisted solely of the pieces she was wearing that she had hired the previous day, she said hastily, 'It's really very small. I only started it recently.' Then she nodded coolly. 'Please don't let me keep you. I expect you want to finish looking round before the sale starts.'

Ignoring her dismissal, he said, 'I've seen everything I want to see. Are you going to bid for the bracelet?'

'Yes, I think so.'

'Then we'd better take our places; the sale is due to start shortly.'

Abby pretended to hesitate. 'Thank you, Mr Lazenby, but really I hardly know you and ...'

He looked amused. 'I assure you I'm perfectly respectable, Miss Stevens. Didn't the auctioneer vouch for me?'

'He merely said that you were an expert on silver,' Abby pointed out drily. 'That doesn't necessarily make you respectable.'

The amused curl on his thin mouth deepened. 'Well, I don't know you either, but I'm willing to take a chance.'

Abby gasped inwardly; if he only knew just how much of a chance he *was* taking! But she merely gave a cool smile as she shrugged and moved towards the sales room. A seat had been reserved for him near the front but to one side, and the enterprising official who had been talking to him earlier must have kept his eye on them, because he had saved Abby a seat next to Lazenby's.

'Do you collect all silver?' Abby asked as they sat down. 'Or do you specialise?'

He began to describe his collection, telling her how he had started with some pieces that had been left to him when he was a boy and these had aroused his interest enough to make a study of the subject. He spoke knowledgeably, so that Abby was interested despite herself. She noticed that he didn't use his hands much to illustrate his words, which was a shame; hands gave away a lot. Hers she kept demurely folded together in her lap.

The sale soon started and she was able to look away from him with some relief; he had the disconcerting habit of keeping his eyes on your face when he talked to you. But she was very aware of him sitting beside her, his wide shoulders taking up more than his fair share of room.

It was the first auction sale Abby had ever been to, and she was surprised that hardly anyone seemed to make any verbal bids, they simply raised a finger or their catalogue. Charles Bradbury had given her some idea of what went on the night before so that she wouldn't make any mistakes, but it still felt odd. He had already been to view the lots for sale and told her about the bracelet, arranged for her to bid for it and buy it, no matter how high it went. 'You're supposed to be rich,' he reminded her. 'If you see something you want, you buy it.'

The silver chalice came up for sale and Lazenby gave a nod so brief that it wasn't much more than a movement of his head. The chalice was knocked down at fourteen thousand pounds. 'Lazenby,' the auctioneer murmured, and the lovely, graceful piece was taken away. He bought two more items before the bracelet was brought out.

Several people bid and the auctioneer paused before Abby raised her hand a little at one thousand, five hundred pounds. Immediately somebody over on the left raised the price and she had to bid again, taking the price to two thousand. It seemed as if there was only the two of them bidding, because the same thing happened again. Confidently Abby raised her hand; Charles Bradbury had said buy it, and he was paying. Bidding with someone else's money, she found, was quite good fun. Her unseen opponent stayed in for a little longer, but eventually the bracelet was knocked down to her for three thousand, two hundred and fifty pounds.

She went out to the office to pay and Lazenby followed. Abby's face was a little flushed, her eyes excited. 'I'm so pleased that I got it!'

He shrugged. 'You can always get what you want if you're willing to pay enough.'

'You think I paid too much for it?'

'It depends how badly you wanted it.'

She raised her head to look at him, lips slightly pouted. 'I wanted it.'

A cynical look came into his eyes. 'And do you always get what you want?'

Abby had been about to say yes, but she changed her mind suddenly and laughed aloud.

'No, of course not. You're quite wrong, you know. Money can't buy everything you want.'

She turned away then, gratified by the quick flame of interest that had come into his cool eyes. She wrote out a cheque for the bracelet and had to fill in a form with her name and address. 'I will be able to take it away with me, won't I?' she asked the cashier. 'I'd like to wear it to the opera tonight.'

'Of course, madam. If you could just wait a few minutes while we have it wrapped for you.' Which was a polite way of giving them time to make sure that her cheque was good. But Charles Bradbury had taken care of all that and she knew there would be no problem. She noticed that Lance Lazenby just signed his name to a form, so evidently he bought quite a lot here.

The bracelet was brought out to her and she slipped it into her bag, then Lance Lazenby came over and escorted her back out into the spring sunshine. He put a hand under her elbow and smiled down at her lazily. 'Shall we continue our talk about our respective collections over lunch?'

Abby lifted a gloved hand and a cruising taxi pulled up beside them. 'I'm afraid I'm busy. Thank you so much for your help, Mr Lazenby. Goodbye.' And with a brief nod she firmly drew her arm away and got into the taxi, closing the door behind her before she leant forward to give the driver the address of her flat.

As the taxi drew away leaving Lance Lazenby alone in the street, Abby sat back with some satisfaction, sure that her fish had taken the bait and swallowed it enough to want more. Charles Bradbury, of course, wouldn't have agreed with her; he would have wanted her to accept the lunch

invitation that Lance Lazenby had been so sure
would be accepted. And he had wanted her to
flaunt her hair. But Abby had insisted on the more
subtle, hard-to-get approach. Let Lazenby get
interested and slowly feed him more; then there
would be a chance of keeping him dangling on her
line. But she was pretty sure that if she threw
herself at him he would soon lose interest.

Clutching the bag with the precious bracelet in it
to her, Abby hurried into her flat and only relaxed
when she had placed it, and the jet jewellery, in the
wall safe. That she was busy had been a lie; she
had nothing to do now until the evening when she
hoped that Lance Lazenby would pick up the clue
she had given him and follow her to the opera. Mr
Bradbury had got her two tickets for *Don
Giovanni*, and as this was the only opera being
performed in London that night, if he wanted to
follow her he wouldn't have too much difficulty.
And then she would be sure that he was really
interested.

Abby spent the rest of the afternoon washing
her hair and generally getting ready, and at seven
her escort arrived. He was a fellow actor named
Ross Newton, tall, muscular, and very good-
looking, with thick curly brown hair and a
fashionable moustache that he thought made him
look older than his twenty-five years. He was also
out of work and glad to act as her escort when
there was the promise of a free meal at the end of
the evening. He looked good in a well-cut evening
suit that Abby had hired for him from the same
place she had got the black mink jacket she was
wearing. Under it she wore a long, deep red jersey
dress which, although it wasn't tight, moved with
her and outlined her tall, slender, almost boyish

figure. The dress also had long sleeves and a
deep-cowl neckline that she could put up as a
loose hood to cover her hair. Most redheads
wouldn't have worn red, but Abby knew from
experience that her particular shade of chestnut
hair had a striking effect when worn with a red
outfit.

When they arrived at the Opera House Abby
was disappointed; there was no sign of Lance
Lazenby. They sat in the stalls and she looked
round as best she could without making it too
obvious that she was doing so, but she couldn't see
his tall figure anywhere. As the house darkened
and the overture began she settled back in her seat
with a little sigh. Perhaps it had been too much to
hope that he would come, he could easily have
something else on that night, but somehow she
had been sure that he was the kind of man who,
when he was interested in a woman, would follow
it up at once, letting nothing get in his way.

Neither Ross nor herself knew much about
opera; as actors they were totally absorbed only
with drama, and after half an hour or so Ross
leaned towards her and whispered, 'Do we have to
stay and listen to the rest of this?'

'Hush!' Rather to her surprise Abby found that
she was enjoying herself and was engrossed in the
music. 'Yes, of course we must.'

Ross grunted and settled down in his seat. Abby
grinned to herself as she realised a little later that
he'd gone to sleep.

When the interval came she nudged him awake
and they went out to the bar for a drink. They sat
on high stools in a quiet corner and started talking
shop, Abby laughing as Ross told her a funny
story about a show he had been in in Edinburgh,

putting on a Scots accent and doing a really good impression of the stage manager there.

'He sounds impossible,' she remarked, and turned towards the bar to pick up her drink. As she did so she glanced into the mirrored wall that lined the back of the bar and her heart missed a beat. Lance Lazenby was leaning his broad shoulders against a pillar a few yards behind her, partly obscured by the people between them. Careful not to let her face betray her, Abby turned back to Ross, took a drink and then said softly, 'Hey, that man I was telling you about—he's here after all.'

'Okay.' Ross, as if given a cue, went into the act they'd agreed on. He leant forward and picked up her hand, played with it while looking admiringly into her eyes. 'Which one?' he asked.

'Tall and dark. Over by the pillar.' Abby smiled back at him as Ross lifted her hand to his lips.

'Okay, got him. He's looking at us now,' he said as if he was making love to her. Letting go her fingers, he put up his hands and gently pushed the hood back off her head so that her hair fell in a rich, tumbling cascade of flame about her shoulders.

Abby sneaked a look at the mirror and saw her victim staring at her, his drink frozen halfway to his mouth, a knocked-out expression on his lean face. But he recovered extremely quickly and Abby had to hastily look away as he carried on lifting his glass, but she could almost have sworn that his hand wasn't quite so steady now.

She was careful not to look towards him again during the interval. Ross continued to flirt with her until the bell rang and they finished their drinks and turned to go back to their seats. There was no sign of Lazenby in the bar and again she couldn't see him in the auditorium. But after the opera, when Abby had collected her jacket from the cloakroom and was walking to where Ross was waiting, she found someone blocking her way and looked up to find Lance Lazenby in front of her.

'Good evening.' He spoke quite casually, then slightly lifted one dark eyebrow when she didn't immediately reply and said, 'It is Miss Stevens, isn't it?'

'Why, yes.' Abby got her breath back and answered, 'I'm sorry, I was just surprised at running into you again, Mr—er—Lazenby.'

'And are you also an opera fan as well as a collector?' His eyes went to her hair and Abby wondered insanely if he was trying to see whether it was natural or dyed.

Luckily she was saved from answering as Ross walked over to them. He put a possessive hand on Abby's arm and looked at Lance Lazenby rather belligerently, 'You okay, Abby?'

'Of course. This is Lance Lazenby. Ross Newton.' Ross had to let go her arm as the two men shook hands. Lazenby, too, was in evening dress, but somehow it seemed to sit better on him than it did on Ross, making him look more lean and powerful. Abby was tall, but both men dwarfed her.

'It's the strangest coincidence,' Abby went on. 'I only met Mr Lazenby this morning, at the sale at Sotheby's. He advised me about this bracelet I bought.' She held up her right arm where the silver bracelet glowed against the dark red cloth of her sleeve.

'It looks—very beautiful.' Lance Lazenby's eyes came up and met hers, held them for a long moment until Abby looked away, her heart beating rather fast. He turned to Ross. 'You're interested in Mozart's operas?'

Abby held her breath, but Ross wasn't a good actor for nothing. He grinned boyishly. 'I'm afraid I know very little about opera; it was Abby who wanted to come.'

'And did you enjoy it?'

'Yes, I did,' Abby answered sincerely. 'Very much.'

'They're doing *The Magic Flute* soon; I'm sure you would like that, too.'

'I'll make a point of going to see it.' She smiled and nodded, turned to go with Ross beside her, but Lazenby moved deliberately to her other side and walked through to the foyer with them.

As they came to the entrance he said, 'I have my car outside. Perhaps you'd care to join me for a meal?'

'Thanks,' Ross said tersely, every inch the possessive boy-friend, 'but we already have a table booked.' He hesitated, then said, 'I'll get a taxi.'

Abby half expected Lazenby to repeat his offer, but he didn't, merely standing silently while they watched Ross go out into the cool night. Then he turned to her. 'When am I going to see you again?' he demanded abruptly.

She gave a little gasp and looked at him with eyes that were genuinely startled. He had his hands in the pockets of his trousers, but his eyes were fixed on her face and Abby had the strangest feeling, as if he was touching her quite freely. She shook her head. 'I'm sorry, Mr Lazenby, but . . .'

'Lance,' he interrupted.

'All right—Lance. As you can see, I'm already dating Ross.'

'Are you engaged to him?'

'Well, no, but . . .'

'Then you're free to go out with me.'

'I would be—if I wanted to.'

'And don't you want to?' He moved a little nearer, his eyes searching her face, resting on her lips. His hard body menacing and powerful.

Abby caught her breath, almost frightened at the degree of masculine arrogance and magnetism he had. Involuntarily she stepped back. Thank God she knew about Sarah Bradbury and was forewarned, otherwise it would be all too easy to fall for him. Looking at him as coolly as she could, she shook her head. 'No, I don't think I do.' Then she left him and went outside to join Ross. A couple of minutes later they found a taxi and were just getting into it when they saw Lazenby come out and leave in a beautiful chauffeur-driven silver Rolls.

The next day her phone rang, and Abby felt no surprise when she heard who it was. Finding out her phone number would have been child's play to a man like Lance Lazenby. Nevertheless she pretended surprise and said, 'How did you find out my number? It's ex-directory.'

'A contact in British Telecom,' he told her laconically. 'Will you have dinner with me tonight?'

'No, I already have a date.'

'Tomorrow, then?'

'No. Look, I told you, I'm going out with Ross and . . .'

'Is he your lover?'

Abby gasped. 'Whether he is or not is of no importance to you, and I . . .'

'On the contrary,' he interrupted smoothly, 'it's starting to become very important to me.'

Even though she refused he continued to ring her, and he sent her flowers; not great bunches or terribly expensive blooms like orchids or roses, but irresistible baskets of anemones, or white violets in a bed of velvet green moss. Abby pretended to hold out for almost two weeks, by the end of which time Charles Bradbury was biting his nails and pleading with her to give in in case she lost him, but she knew what she was doing and hung on, then agreed to let Lance take her to see a performance of *The Magic Flute*. 'But only this once,' Abby cautioned when she accepted. 'And only because Ross gets bored at the opera.'

'Of course,' he agreed smoothly. But as Abby put the phone down they both knew, for entirely different reasons, that the game had begun.

CHAPTER THREE

THERE was no question of Abby meeting Lance Lazenby at Covent Garden as she'd suggested; he insisted on coming to pick her up at her flat, so she more or less had to invite him in for a drink. As before, he was wearing an impeccably cut evening suit under a black overcoat because it was a wet night. When Abby took it from him to hang in the cupboard by the door, he turned and looked round the flat, taking in the expensively modern, but not too progressive, furniture and décor that had come with the flat. The few good paintings on the walls, the Chippendale dining table and chairs and the other antique pieces had been provided by Charles Bradbury to back up the story they had concocted for her to use as a background.

She expected him to compliment her on her taste, but instead he said, 'This room suits your personality.'

'Really? In what way?'

'It's modern and elegant, yet with a sympathy for the past. Perhaps even with what are now considered to be old-fashioned ideals.'

Abby smiled. 'What can I get you to drink?'

'Gin and tonic, please.' He came to stand disconcertingly close as she poured the drinks. 'Does my observation amuse you?'

That too was disconcertingly close; Abby had indeed been amused that he should find so much of her in a room that had not one single possession of her own. Lightly she said, 'Only that you think you know so much of my personality from such a short acquaintance.'

'Am I so wrong, then?'

Abby handed him his drink and moved away to sit in a chair. She was wearing her own black velvet evening gown tonight, the one she had worn last in that play in Bristol. Her hair she had taken up to emphasise the fine bone structure of her face and the length of her white neck. She knew that she looked good; looking good was part of her stock in trade and she wasn't vain about it, but she knew how to use it. 'I'm not in the least old-fashioned,' she told him calmly, but with a hint of coolness in her voice.

He caught it and smiled. 'I beg your pardon. I should have realised that old-fashioned is a dirty word to the current generation. Shall I say then that you value what is good from the past?' He came to sit in the chair opposite hers, casually crossing one long leg over the other.

'If you wish, but you'd be quite wrong. This is a furnished flat, so I haven't chosen either the décor or the furniture, and the antique pieces and paintings were left to me by a relative, so you see there's really nothing of my personality in it at all.'

For the first time genuine amusement showed in his grey eyes, and Abby felt as if she had scored the first hit in their verbal fencing match. Perhaps he felt it too, for he said softly, 'Touché.' And the strange thing was that she hadn't meant to say it; she'd meant to acknowledge the room as her own work instead of denying it with a half lie that was close to the truth. But he had needled her into wanting to score off him, to show him that his easy assumptions were wrong. But perhaps, looking at his sardonically amused mouth, she hadn't scored after all, perhaps that was what he had intended all along. She would have to watch herself more closely, Abby decided; she had come dangerously close to under-rating her opponent and that would never do. Not in this game and with this man.

'And why is that?' he was asking blandly.

'I haven't lived here very long. I only came to London a few weeks ago.'

'You haven't been here before?'

'Oh, yes, dozens of times. But I've never lived here before.'

'Then you must let me show you around, introduce you to people.'

'Thank you.' Abby drained her glass and smiled at him charmingly. 'But I already have Ross to do all that.'

'Ah yes. The good-looking Mr Ross Newton who doesn't like opera.' He glanced at his watch and stood up.

'Which is why tonight I'm with the good-looking Mr Lazenby who does,' Abby parried.

Again that flash of amusement. Crossing the room, he took her hand and pulled her to her feet. He was very close, only a few inches away. 'Lance,' he corrected her.

'Lance,' she agreed, her heart beginning to sound in her chest. She would have to think of him as that now, not the Lazenby man. He was so close. Was he going to kiss her or not? Could he hear her heart beating as he stood looking down at her so enigmatically, his eyes searching her face?

But he gave a sort of sigh and said, 'You're exquisitely lovely.' Then he smiled, the smile that didn't reach his eyes. 'But you already know that.'

'Do I?'

'Oh, yes. Girls who don't even blink when they're paid such lavish compliments are perfectly aware of their own beauty.' He stepped away from her, looked around. 'It's time we were going. Have you a coat?'

He helped her on with her mink jacket, his touch impersonal, then shrugged himself into his overcoat. It was pouring with rain outside, but his chauffeur was on the lookout and quickly came with a huge umbrella to hold over them for the short distance to the car.

Abby had never been in a privately-owned Rolls before and it was difficult not to show it. She wanted to stroke the leather upholstery and play with all the gadgets: the telephone and miniature bar, the buttons set into the arm of her seat, and the television set incorporated into a console with a radio and cassette player. There was also what seemed a small library of cassettes, but it was too dark to read their titles; mostly opera, Abby presumed.

The Magic Flute was easy enough to follow because she'd done her homework earlier, but she found her concentration slipping. She was far too conscious of the man beside her. They were in the best seats, of course, and there was plenty of room, but her shoulder still touched his sleeve and the contact seemed to burn into her so that she wasn't at ease. Not that she wanted to be at ease with him, to be so might make her lose her guard and she was sure that if she made even the slightest slip he would pounce on it; not because he suspected her or anything, but just because he was too intelligent not to notice. Her programme slipped from her fingers and she moved to retrieve it before it fell to the floor. Lance did the same, and their fingers touched. Taken unawares, Abby couldn't control the tremor of emotion that ran through her. She looked up and their eyes met. For a moment that seemed to go on for ever they were alone in the crowded theatre, with only the music swirling around them. Deliberately his grip tightened on her hand, his fingers strong and forceful, then he let her go and the moment was past.

During the interval they went to the bar where Lance had drinks waiting and they talked on safe, uncontroversial subjects, but after the opera he took her to a restaurant for a meal and here returned to a more personal level.

'Where did you live before you came to London?' he asked as they sipped their aperitifs.

Abby shrugged. 'Nowhere in particular. I lived with an elderly aunt who loved to travel. She used to borrow second houses or holiday villas from her friends and we stayed in them until they wanted to use them or until she got the travel bug again.'

'Used to? You used the past tense.'

'Yes, she died earlier this year, when we were staying at a bungalow belonging to one of her friends in the Canary Islands.'

'So you were free to live in London?' he remarked, the dryness in his voice implying a host of things, none of them complimentary.

Abby's chin came up. 'It wasn't a question of being free. I could have come here at any time if I'd wanted to. But I happened to enjoy being with my aunt; she was wonderful company and great fun to be with. We had some really good times together.' Abby thought she'd played that rather well—she could almost see this imaginery and exciting-to-be-with aunt in her mind's eye.

'I beg your pardon,' Lance said gravely. 'But it was after she died that you came to London?'

'Yes.'

'Why here and not some other country or town?'

Abby took a minute to think that one out, then answered in a slightly lost voice that riveted his eyes to her face, 'I had nowhere else to go.'

He opened his mouth to follow this up, but luckily the head waiter came to show them to their table, and after they were seated, Abby changed the subject. 'And you? I take it you live in London?'

'Yes, near Hyde Park.'

'And do you work in London?' Abby opened her evening bag and turned on the miniature cassette recorder that Bradbury had given her while she pretended to look for her handkerchief. Not that she expected to glean anything, but they would be able to see how well it worked. 'You do work, don't you?' she added as if it was an afterthought.

He gave a small smile. 'Yes, of course. I work in the City.'

'Oh—the City. That can cover a multitude of sins, can't it?'

'Of sins?' he asked in a careful, probing tone.

Abby smiled innocently in return. 'It's just an expression. Of occupations, then?'

'Yes, I suppose it can. I'm an executive in a holding company.'

'An executive! That sounds terribly grand. Tell me, what does an executive do? Does he execute people?'

Lance laughed drily. 'I suppose you could say that was one of his many functions.' He leaned forward and reached across the table, imprisoning her hand under his. 'Are you trying to make fun of me, Abby?'

To her annoyance her hand trembled a little. To cover it she said mockingly, 'Why, don't you like to be made fun of? Are you so serious?'

'Not in the least. I can enjoy a joke with anyone. But I should like to know why you find me amusing.'

'I don't. You're mistaken.' Abby took her hand away, afraid that he would feel it tremble again, not liking the turn the conversation had taken. But he didn't pursue the matter, turning the topic back to the opera and telling her about Salzburg, Mozart's birthplace, and the music festivals that were held there.

They stayed on safe subjects until after the meal, then he asked her to dance. It was the usual pocket-handkerchief floor to be found in most clubs, designed as an excuse for people to have to get close; not that most of the dancers seemed to need an excuse, some of them couldn't have got much closer if they'd started making love while they were dancing. Abby moved into Lance's arms, conscious of his height and width as she'd never been with Ross, although he was bigger if anything. There was something about Lance that Ross lacked, perhaps it was the fact that Lance was almost ten years older and had more self-confidence, was sure of his own ability to succeed in everything he did and to always get what he wanted. Perhaps it was only that he had more inborn arrogance and pride.

As they danced Abby wondered just what it was that Bradbury had heard about him. He had been rather vague, mentioning bribes to get orders and share juggling, whatever that might mean. She stole a glance under her lashes at Lance's face. Would he really stoop so low to further his own ends? His face was cold and withdrawn and there was a harshness about his mouth. Yes, the man wouldn't hesitate to take any steps he thought necessary to get what he wanted, just as he hadn't hesitated to ruin poor Sarah Bradbury in revenge for the one time that he hadn't succeeded. And it was her job to try to expose him, to show him up for what he was! Abby's hand shook as she only now realised the temerity of the task she'd undertaken. She would have to be careful, so careful. Because if he ever found out . . . Her hand shook again and Lance glanced down at her, the harsh lines leaving his mouth as he smiled lazily.

Pulling her a little closer, he said, 'When are you going to come out with me again?'

Abby determinedly pushed herself back into her role of sophisticated lady and gave him a cool smile. 'It was just to see the opera, remember?'

His hand slid down low on her waist, deliberately holding her against him. 'And is opera our only wavelength?' he asked softly.

Stifling a gasp, Abby moved away. 'I'm dating Ross; you know that.'

'Then get rid of him.'

This time Abby did gasp at the peremptoriness of the order. 'For you? Why on earth should I?'

'Because he isn't the right man for you.'

'And you think you are, I suppose.' Anger flickered in her voice.

'Perhaps. I could certainly give you a lot more than he can.'

The anger increased as she retorted, 'I'm not interested in a man for what he can give me, only for what he is. And I'd like to go now, please.'

She tried to pull away, but he kept hold of her, made her go on dancing. 'Your eyes flash like the finest emeralds when you're angry. Say you'll have dinner with me tomorrow?'

'No!'

'Lunch, then?'

'I've told you, no. I—I don't want to see you again.'

'Oh, yes you do, Abby. Give up the pretence.'

Abby's heart almost stopped with fear. 'What—what do you mean?' she stammered.

'Only that you're not as emotionless as you pretend to be behind that cool, elegant façade. What else would I mean?'

She felt faint with relief and slowly began to function again. 'Why do you say that?'

Lifting his hand, he put it on her neck and gently traced the long outline of her throat with his thumb. 'Because you tremble every time I touch you, my beautiful lady,' he told her softly.

The music stopped and they came to a standstill, though Abby was hardly aware of it as she stared up at him, lips parted, her eyes searching his face. But he merely gave that small, unreadable smile of his and, putting his arm round her waist, led her back to their table.

As they sat down Abby tried to work out how to play the situation and wished heartily that she had a script to work to. Nothing was turning out quite as she'd expected it to. She had meant to keep Lance at arm's length for quite a bit longer, but he had taken the game under his own control with a vengeance. And when he had accused her of pretending it had really unnerved her. Picking up her glass, Abby looked at him over its rim. Did she really tremble every time he touched her? If she did it was out of a mixture of tension and revulsion. She didn't want to be touched by Lance Lazenby, not when she'd seen what he'd done to Charles Bradbury's daughter. She must keep reminding herself of that, never let it stray far from the surface of her mind. And it helped, it certainly helped.

Calm again, she said, 'You said you were something in the City; does that mean that you know about stocks and shares?'

'Quite a bit. Why?' He took out a thin, dark cigar from a gold case and lit it from the lighter incorporated into the case.

'My aunt left me a few shares and her solicitor has advised me to have an expert look over them. He seems to think it might be better to re-invest. I wondered if you might know of someone I could go to for advice.'

'I know of a great many people. I'll give you some names and you can pick out a couple to consult.'

'Two?'

'It's just as well to have a second opinion with one's finances as with one's health. Don't you agree?'

'I really hadn't thought about it, but it sounds a good idea. Is that what you do?'

'Take advice from two people, do you mean?'

'Yes.'

Lance shook his head decisively. 'I make my own decisions. And if I make a mistake it's my responsibility and no one else's.'

'But you don't often make mistakes?' Abby goaded.

'No, not about the stock market—or about women,' he added deliberately.

They left soon afterwards and when they got to her flat Lance insisted on seeing her up to it, leaving the tired chauffeur yawning over the steering wheel. At the door he took her key from her and unlocked the door. Abby stood waiting, wondering what he would do; there was such a choice of things he could do now: try to persuade her to let him stay the night, go into a passionate goodnight kiss, start trying to get her to agree to go out with him again, or just, but highly unlikely, shake hands and go.

In the event, he did none of those things. He merely said, 'I'll see that those names you wanted are sent round to you. Goodnight, Abby.' His hand came up and he gently traced the outline of her lips. 'You're so lovely. So like . . .' He broke off abruptly. 'Tonight was very special for me.' Taking his hand away, he looked at her intently for a long moment, then turned and strode away.

The list of share experts was sent round to the flat the following morning, together with a great spray of budding white lilac, enough to fill three vases and fill the flat with its scent. At lunchtime Abby took the list and the cassette tape with her when she went to meet Charles Bradbury at a small, unobtrusive restaurant in north London, well away from Lance's area.

'You did well,' Bradbury congratulated her when she recounted what had happened. 'It will be interesting to know who his friends are, who he does business through. This list should be a great help in that. The tape worked all right?'

'Yes, I played it back and it's a bit muffled in places, but you can hear it if you turn the volume right up.'

'Good. Good. Here's the list I've made up of

shares your makebelieve aunt might have had. You can phone a couple of these names he's given you and read the list out to them, ask for their advice. Better ask for it in writing. Oh, and don't forget to mention Lazenby's name.'

'Won't they want to see the actual portfolio?' Abby objected.

'It's highly unlikely. You wouldn't have the shares in your own home, they'd be with your solicitor or in your bank.'

'Oh, I see.' Abby definitely saw that she knew nothing about the way the rich half of the population handled their money. 'Which two shall I phone?'

Bradbury picked up the list and studied it. 'This one ... and yes, I think this one. It should be interesting to see just what they advise. They're both deeply involved with one of Lazenby's subsidiary companies. Now,' he held out his hand, 'what bills have you got for me?'

Abby passed over the invoices she had received from the jewel and fur hire place along with ordinary domestic bills. Bradbury totted them up and then wrote out a cheque to cover them, plus fifty pounds more which he described as petty cash. He had insisted from the start that the flat and everything else should be in her name so that Lance wouldn't be suspicious if he ever tried to check up on Abby—a sensible safety precaution.

They discussed the situation a little longer and he agreed when Abby suggested she'd better go out with Ross a few times more for appearances' sake, then they each left the restaurant and went their separate ways.

She contacted Ross and the following night they went to the theatre together, both of them fully awake as they watched their peers up on the stage, afterwards having a friendly but heated argument all through their meal as they pulled the production to pieces. Ross took her back to the flat and came in for a drink. Abby told him to help himself and went to close the curtains. As she did so something caught her eye and she glanced down at the open space in front of the building where the residents parked their cars. There was a sleek red sports car parked down there that she hadn't seen before. Then she realised what had caught her eye; there was someone in it smoking a cigarette, she could see the small red glow as whoever it was drew on it.

'How long are you going to be here?' Ross was asking.

Abby closed the curtains to and turned round. She shrugged. 'I'm not sure. It depends on various circumstances.'

'Well, it can't be bad, living in a place like this. It sure beats the hell out of my digs.'

Sitting beside him on the settee, Abby kicked off her shoes and tucked her feet under her. 'What's wrong with your bed-sit?'

'Mice,' he said succintly.

'Ugh! You poor thing.'

'I certainly am. You should feel extremely sorry for me. Let me describe my bed-sit to you.' Putting an arm round her, Ross drew her comfortably closer to him and soon had her gurgling with laughter as he grossly exaggerated all the defects of his room near Victoria Station. 'There is one advantage, though,' he told her in mock seriousness. 'You don't put on weight living there, because whenever a train goes by everything starts to shake and it acts like one of those slimming machines that vibrates your fat away.'

'You idiot!' Abby gave him a playful punch in his ribs. 'I happen to know your landlady dotes on you.'

He laughed and then looked at her more seriously. 'You know, Abby, we get along okay, don't we? And you're certainly something to have around.' Leaning forward, he kissed her lingeringly. 'Are you going to make me sleep with all those mice or are we going to get to know each other much, much better?' And he kissed her again.

Abby let him kiss her; she liked it and she liked the sensual feelings it aroused in her. Ross was nice, she liked him and felt comfortable with him. Too comfortable. Gently she pushed him away. She was a girl of her times and had no sexual hang-ups. She was free to say yes if she wanted to and equally free to say no if she didn't. And now, strangely enough, because Ross was everything most girls wanted in a man, she found that she didn't want to have sex with him.

He raised an eyebrow. 'No?'

She shook her head. 'No, Ross. Sorry.'

'That's okay. I'd better be getting along, then. Back to the mice.'

'Maybe you'll find your fairy godmother waiting there for you,' Abby said lightly.

Ross grimaced. 'To turn it into a pad like this? Somehow I don't think so.'

When his taxi came, Abby watched him go from the window and noticed that the man in the sports car was still there. And he was there again a few nights later when she once more went out with Ross and he came back for a drink. This time he didn't proposition her, but he didn't let his disappointment mar their friendship; he was just as natural as he'd been before.

During these few days Abby had contacted the two financial experts and they had promised to let her have their written advice as soon as possible. When she had first spoken to them they had treated her just as an ordinary client, pushing her off on to some junior, and it was almost funny the way she had been hastily transferred to the man at the top the moment she had mentioned that Lance had recommended them. But it gave her a useful insight into the amount of power he wielded.

He didn't phone her himself, call round, or send her any more flowers, which at first she found intriguing but then started to worry her. What if she'd put him off? Mr Bradbury would have spent all that money for nothing. She tried to keep calm, going out during the day to art galleries and auction sales, or shopping, and in the evening catching up on films, television programmes and reading; doing all the things she hadn't before had time for during her busy career. But after a week the fear began to grow into a certainty, that Lance Lazenby had slipped off her line.

Then, just as she had got to the nail-biting stage, her doorbell rang one evening and he was there.

Abby opened the door and gazed at him, too taken by surprise at first to speak. He was dressed in a dark business suit, his hands as usual in his pockets, stretching the material tight across his hips. 'Hallo, Abby.'

'What—what do you want?' She could read nothing in his face and it unnerved her.

'This.' Taking his hands out of his pockets, he stepped quickly into the room and shouldered the door shut behind him. Then he pulled her roughly into his arms and kissed her.

There was nothing comfortable in the way Lance kissed; there was no gentleness about it, only a hard possessiveness that demanded, and got, a response. At first Abby was taken by surprise, then anger filled her at his high-handedness and she tried to pull away, but his hand was in her hair, tilting her head back so that she couldn't move. But then she was caught by the fierce onslaught of his mouth and she no longer wanted to move. There was a mastery in his embrace that she had never experienced before and she submitted to it in bewilderment, her lips parting under his and her arms going up around his neck as something inside her seemed to ignite and burst into flame. She gasped and her mouth moved under his, taking now as much as it gave, her body filled with a hot flame of desire.

And then, just as deliberately as he had begun to kiss her, Lance let her go and stepped back, leaving her gazing at him wide-eyed and open-mouthed, overwhelmed by a feeling of desolation and loss.

'I've been wanting to do that since the first moment I saw you,' he said unevenly, his breath a little faster than usual.

Abby gulped and tried to pull herself together, shattered by the impact of his kiss. 'I—I think I need a drink,' she stammered.

Lance laughed. 'That makes two of us—definitely!'

He went over to the drinks tray and Abby, finding that her legs felt suddenly weak, went to sit on the settee, then hastily changed her mind and moved to the safety of a chair. My God, she thought, did he always kiss like that? No wonder poor Sarah Bradbury had fallen for him. Remembering Sarah helped; by the time he came over with the drink she had managed to regain some degree of composure and get back into the part she was playing. Not that her response to his kiss had been part of the act—that had been an entirely natural reaction.

Lance stood looking down at her with a rather rueful smile. 'I'm sorry—I took you by surprise.'

'You did rather.' Abby took the glass from him and tried to still the beating of her heart.

'I've been away,' he told her abruptly. He didn't sit down, but paced restlessly about the room as if he felt it confined him. Then he set down his glass rather hard so that it clattered against the polished surface of the table, and stood towering over her. 'I couldn't get you out of my mind. I want you to give up seeing Ross Newton. Will you do that?'

He seemed to loom over her like some dark bird of prey, like a hawk waiting to pounce. Constrained by it, Abby got to her feet and moved towards the window, trying to still the agitation in her mind. This was what she'd been aiming for, what she and Charles Bradbury had so hoped to achieve, but now that the moment had come she found herself incredibly reluctant to accept it. Some small inner voice told her to reject him, to get out and have done with this man.

Behind her, Lance repeated urgently, 'Will you give him up? Will you?'

Slowly she turned to face him, her cheeks very pale. 'Yes, all right.'

'My dear!' He stepped quickly towards her and Abby's heart surged as she thought that he was going to kiss her again, but he merely caught hold of her hands and carried them to his lips. Then a frown came into his grey eyes. 'Please don't look like that.'

'Like—like what?'

'So scared. You're not afraid of me, are you?' Still holding her hands, he drew her back into the room.

'N-no, of course not.' Abby tried to smile but it didn't quite come off. 'But you do rather—take one's breath away.'

Lance laughed softly. 'My poor darling! But you see, when I want something very, very much, then I'm afraid I do tend to pursue it rather determinedly.'

That wasn't how Abby would have put it; she would have described it in far stronger terms, and wondered with a shiver what would have happened if she'd said no. But she knew that Lance wasn't the kind of man to take no for an answer and was glad that she'd capitulated and would never find out. Now all she had to worry about was what he would do now that she'd said yes.

Leading her to the settee, he sat down and pulled her down beside him. Idly he began to toy with her fingers as he said, 'It's Saturday tomorrow. Will you spend the day with me? There's an antiques fair a couple of hours' drive from London that I think you'd enjoy.'

'Yes, I'd like that.'

'Good. Maybe we'll have dinner at a country inn somewhere on the way back.'

And then what? Abby wondered wildly. Will you expect to go to bed with me? Have I said yes to that, too? Her hand shook and he stopped playing with her fingers, looked quickly up into her face.

'You're trembling. Did I scare you so much?'

'Perhaps. Just a little,' she admitted. 'You were so insistent that I give up Ross.'

His face hardened. 'I don't share my women, Abby.'

Quick anger flared in her green eyes and she snatched her hand away. 'I'm not your woman!'

She didn't know what reaction to expect from him after that, but it certainly wasn't the cool amusement that curled his mouth so mockingly. 'Of course you're not,' he said soothingly, at the same time putting up a hand to cup her chin, his eyes lingering on her mouth as he bent to kiss her.

Abby got quickly to her feet before he could do so. 'I'm rather tired,' she said shortly, her chin coming up. 'I'd like you to leave now, please.'

He gave her a surprised, contemplative look, but to her relief, got obediently to his feet. 'Of course.' He was all concern. 'I should have realised. When may I call for you tomorrow?'

'About nine-thirty? Will that give us time?'

'It will be fine. Till tomorrow, then.' Fortunately he only kissed her lightly on the forehead, but he let his hand linger in her hair, idly running its rich silkiness through his fingers. 'You have such beautiful hair. And such an unusual shade. I've only ever encountered it once before.'

'Oh?' Abby tried to keep her voice casual. 'When was that? Was it on a girl?'

Immediately a set mask came down over his features and he took his hand away. 'It was so long ago I can't remember. Goodnight, Abby. Don't bother to see me out.'

'Goodnight.'

Only when she'd heard the door close safely behind him did some of the tension fall away.

Abby felt as if she'd been on the stage for hours, playing some really gruelling part like Lady Macbeth. Going into the bathroom, she turned on the tap and patted cold water against her hot face, then went into the sitting-room to pour herself another drink, almost collapsing into a chair. So much for her ability to be detached from the part she was playing and not get involved. If it went on like this she'd be a nervous wreck by the time it was over.

Leaning back, Abby set herself to carefully go over what had occurred to see if she could glean anything from it that might be useful in the future. The first and most important thing of course was that sexually Lance was quite devastating. The memory of his kiss still made her feel hot and confused, something that hadn't happened to her for quite some time. She liked to keep her relationships with men on a cool and friendly basis so that there were never any hard feelings when they split, but if just one of his kisses could have an impact on her like that ... Whew! It was a whole new ball game. And again she wondered just what he wanted from her. Okay, so he'd left straightaway when she'd asked him to tonight, but that didn't mean that she was going to be able to hold him at arm's length indefinitely. Sipping her drink, Abby remembered the autocratic way he'd said that he didn't share his women—and the mockingly amused way he'd smiled when she'd protested. He'd been going to kiss her again then. Abby's hand froze in mid-air as understanding hit her. Lance had laughed because he knew full well that his first kiss had sexually aroused her, and that he only had to do it again to make her realise what he already knew full well: that she was

already his woman, held in thrall by his sheer
masculine domination.

Or so he thought? Angrily Abby finished her
drink and got to her feet, determined to exert her
own personality, to stand apart from the character
she was playing and not let him get to her. And if
she ever found herself in danger of submitting to
his will, she need only remember what Lance had
done to poor Sarah Bradbury. While she remembered that she would be safe from him.
Crossing to the phone, she dialled Charles
Bradbury's number and told him the good news.

Lance called for her punctually the next
morning with a basket of lily-of-the-valley for her
in his hand. 'You look marvellous,' he told her.
'You must have had a good long sleep.'

Abby smiled in return, glad that it didn't show
that after he had left she had gone out to meet
Charles Bradbury, who had given her a very
interesting gold pen to plant on Lance. Outwardly
it looked like an ordinary but expensively made
ballpoint with an LCD clock and Lance's initials
on it, but concealed inside it was a minute bug that
could transmit over quite a long distance. Abby
didn't ask who would be on the receiving end, that
was none of her business, all she had to do was
find a suitable opportunity to give it to Lance.

She was wearing a pale green suit with a very good
label which, along with the Gucci handbag she
carried, had been purchased at less than a quarter of
their original cost at a little shop tucked away in a
side street in Knightsbridge where all the local rich
women sold their last season's haute couture
outfits, or clothes they'd bought on impulse and
were a mistake. Cleaned, and with the latest
accessories, the clothes looked just as good as new.

'I've left my chauffeur behind today,' Lance told her. 'Do you mind?'

'No, of course not.' Abby tried to keep her voice warm, but it slipped a little at the thought of being entirely alone with him all day. As they came out of the building, she looked round, expecting to see the Rolls, but Lance put a hand under her elbow and to her stunned surprise led her over to a low-slung red sports car, its long, sleek lines gleaming in the sun. A car she'd seen before, parked outside the flats with a man sitting in it smoking as he waited, waited to see if Ross would spend the night with her? Abby put the thought aside to examine later, but was filled with exultation that Lance had cared enough to do so. 'This is your car?'

'Yes. Do you like sports cars?'

'Very much.'

He opened the door for her and she climbed in, revealing quite a lot of leg as she did so because of the low seats. The car was new and the rich smell of the leather upholstery came pleasantly to her nostrils. 'How fast does it go?' she asked as Lance got in beside her.

He grinned. 'A hundred and fifty. But the speed limit's seventy in this country, remember?'

Abby wrinkled her nose. 'Don't you ever feel like breaking the law?'

'Not just for the hell of it, no. But if it was something that really mattered and breaking the law was the only way . . .' he shrugged, 'then I'd have no hesitation.'

After one glance at his profile Abby quickly looked away. Her question had been quite innocent, without anything behind it, but it had inadvertently given her another insight into his character.

'How about you?' Lance was asking.

She laughed. 'No, but if I had this lovely machine in my hands I'd certainly be tempted to.'

'Do you drive?'

'I have a licence, but I've never had a car of my own.'

'I suppose you drove your aunt's?'

Abby just stopped herself from saying, 'Whose?' Instead she shook her head. 'She didn't own one either. But we quite often hired one when we were abroad or in the country.'

'Which countries did you visit?'

Remembering the background she'd worked out with Mr Bradbury, Abby named a few places and then changed the subject by asking him about himself. His background was much as she had expected, very upper middle class, good public school, Oxford and then the City. A combination that was guaranteed to turn out a man who was outstanding at what he did, whether it was good or evil.

'Do you have any family?' she asked.

'A married sister and a couple of nephews. They live in Yorkshire and I go up to see them a few times a year. Usually at Christmas, that kind of thing. But small doses of domesticity are enough for me.'

'You're not the marrying type?' Abby asked lightly.

Lance glanced at her and smiled. 'I don't know, I've never tried it. It's other people's domesticity I can't stand.' He paused as he pulled out to overtake a slow-moving lorry. 'How about you? Haven't you ever been tempted to settle down?'

'Marriage is an institution,' Abby answered flippantly. 'And who wants to live in an institution?'

He laughd in real amusement. 'You've been reading too many feminist magazines.'

'Maybe coming to live in London and taking the flat is my way of settling down,' Abby said—adding truthfully as her thoughts went back over seasons spent with touring companies in Britain and abroad, living in cheap digs in one town and another until they all merged into one grubby memory, 'I've certainly had enough travelling around to last me a lifetime.'

'You said that as though you meant it.' Lance flicked on his indicators as they turned left off a roundabout and joined the M4 motorway, heading west. 'How about boy-friends?' he asked casually. 'None that you've felt like marrying?'

'I've never stayed in one place long enough to find out. And you? You've obviously had plenty of experience with women.'

His lips curved into a small smile. 'You think so, do you?'

'I know so,' she answered steadily. 'Haven't you ever wanted to marry one of them?'

His hands gripped the wheel as his profile hardened. He didn't answer at once and the silence began to be heavy between them, but at length he said shortly, 'Once. Long ago.'

'What happened?'

'She was killed, driving a car like this. My car. She'd taken it for a joy-ride. Which is why I'll never let you drive it,' he added abruptly. 'So don't ask.'

'I wasn't going to.'

'Yes, you were. You'd love to get your hands on it.'

Which was quite true; Abby would have given her right arm for one like this. But that wasn't in the part. Pretending to be annoyed, she said, 'If I wanted to drive a car like this I could go out tomorrow and buy one.'

'Ah, yes, I was forgetting that. So you could.' Again he gave that economical smile, then deliberately changed the subject.

They arrived at the antiques fair near Oxford just after eleven and spent a pleasant couple of hours wandering round the stalls. Abby stopped to admire a pretty tortoiseshell box with engraved silver mounts and Lance immediately bought it for her.

'But I can't accept that,' she protested.

His eyebrows went up in surprise. 'Nonsense. It will do to keep some of your collection of jewellery in.'

His surprise served as a warning. Perhaps in the kind of circles he moved in it was customary to give women expensive presents.

They had lunch at a hotel overlooking the Thames. Although it was still early in the year there were already plenty of boats on the river, small pleasure craft mostly, with a few big sightseeing boats crowded with tourists taking advantage of the spring sunshine.

'Do you sail?' Lance asked her as Abby watched a small, red-sailed dinghy tacking across the river.

'I've done a little. I used to have a boy-friend who was mad keen on it. He had a Mirror class dinghy and he used to take it down to the coast most weekends. It was great fun.'

'What happened to the boy-friend?'

Lance had spoken lightly enough, but there was something in his voice which made Abby realise that she'd answered without thinking too much about it. And she'd spoken the truth, out of her own experience. Hastily she tried to think whether it was out of character of the part she was playing, and decided not. She smiled. 'The sailing proved to be more exciting than the boy-friend,' adding, for safety's sake, 'Of course, I was quite young then. Only about eighteen. And you—do you like sailing?'

He nodded. 'I have a yacht, but unfortunately there never seems to be enough time to spend on it. The most I seem to manage is a few weeks in the summer.'

'Where do you keep it—on the coast?'

'No, it has a permanent mooring in the marina at Monte Carlo. I prefer to do my sailing in summer waters.'

Abby remembered a television programme she'd seen of the fantastic motor yachts at Monte Carlo, and gulped. Her kind of sailing and his had no comparison.

After lunch Lance drove to Blenheim Palace and they walked round the huge house that a grateful nation had given to John Churchill, Duke of Marlborough, after the Battle of Blenheim. Lance dispensed with the services of a guide and took her round himself, telling her the history of the house and much about the pieces in it. His knowledge of the antique furniture, pictures and ornaments was little short of expert.

'How do you know so much about the house?' Abby asked in awe.

Lance grinned. 'I'm cheating really. I came here so often when I was a student that I know the place inside out.'

After Blenheim he took her to Oxford itself and Abby listened in fascination as he took her round the ancient town, pointing out the landmarks and making her climb to the top of the tower in the High Street, so that she could see the whole of Oxford laid out before her and count the tall, ornate spires of all the churches and colleges.

'That's my old college, Christ Church,' he pointed out to her. 'The tower over the gateway is called Tom Tower.'

Afterwards he took her there, exchanging a few words with a top-hatted man guarding the gate, who recognised him instantly. Stepping through the arched entrance of Tom Gate was like stepping into another world. All the noise of the busy city streets was left behind and there was a quiet in the Quadrangle that seemed as mellow and friendly as the beautiful old stone buildings themselves. Lance showed her St Frideswide's Chapel, the library, a small museum which was holding an exhibition of ex-student Lewis Carroll's works, and all the other parts of the building open to the public. And every time Lance met anyone he had known, from don down to college servant, he was greeted with smiles of genuine pleasure and interested questions about his health and wellbeing, everyone seeming glad to see him. He introduced Abby to them all and she had her hand vigorously shaken a dozen times as she was looked over with curiosity and interest.

'We don't see enough of you,' one elderly don told Lance. 'Come and have tea with me in my rooms.' So they went, and Abby sat quietly in a comfortable chair by the bow window as Lance and his old tutor talked on subjects way above her head. She sipped her tea from a delicate porcelain cup, half listening half watching the students across the quadrangle below her window. It was a world that was quite new to her, quite outside her experience, and as she watched Abby began to realise just how much she had missed by not going to university. Not just the learning, but the opportunity to be a part of an ancient tradition and to have the privilege of living among such old and beautiful buildings. To wake every morning and see and share in such timelessness.

They said goodbye to their host and walked down to the river, its waters coruscating red and gold in the setting sun. Abby was subdued, walking silently along beside Lance until he took her arm and tucked it in his. 'Penny for them,' he said lightly.

'What?'

'You're miles away. I'm sorry, you must have found the college boring.'

'Good heavens, no! Quite the opposite. In fact my thoughts were right here. I was wishing that I could have had—all this.' She waved her arm in a gesture that took in the river, the college and the town.

'Didn't you have the opportunity to go to university?'

'Oh, I wasn't clever enough. And besides ...' Abby almost said that she was crazy on acting by then, but managed to recover in time, 'I'd had enough of school by the time I left.'

'University is hardly like school,' Lance pointed out.

'No, but you don't realise that at the time. Not if you don't have anyone to tell you.'

Lance gave her a strange look and Abby was afraid that he would pursue the matter, ask her where she had been to school and that kind of thing, but, fortunately, he merely nodded and suggested they go back to the car.

They had dinner at a small country restaurant where candlelight threw shadows among beams blackened by time and applewood logs on the open fire threw a sweetly resinous scent into the room. The food was beautifully cooked and served, making it the kind of meal that would have been perfect if Abby had been with anyone else, if she hadn't to be constantly on her guard and growing ever more tense as she worried about what would happen when they got back to London.

Lance seemed in no hurry; they had liqueurs after the meal and he lit a cigar, settling back in his chair as he told her about his years in Oxford. Abby smiled, nodded and asked questions, but she gradually grew more abstracted, her hands clasped together under the table. Hands were always a dead give-away, and she didn't want him to see that she was nervous. There was nothing nervous about Lance, his hands were rock-steady as he casually talked and smoked the cigar, although he once or twice gave her rather penetrating glances from under his dark, slightly arched brows.

It was already dark when they left to drive back to London, a fine night with stars set high in the cloudless sky.

'Would you like some music?' he asked.

'Please.' Abby selected a cassette and Lance inserted it in the machine. She sat back in her seat, grateful that she didn't have to make conversation. Lance lit another cigar from the lighter on the dashboard and smoked as they drove along, his window a little open to let out the smoke. He was a good driver, confidently manipulating the car, his hands resting lightly on the wheel, not gripping it in nervous tension as some people did. Abby felt perfectly safe and confident of his ability. Which left her free to worry about what would happen when they got back to her flat.

Which was strange for her. Usually she felt quite capable of handling any situation in which she found herself, or any man she was with. But Lance was different, she'd never met anyone like him before. She tried to analyse him, putting together all the facts she knew, but found that she only became more confused. She knew that he was spiteful from what he had done to Sarah Bradbury, and that he was ruthless—he had said himself that if he wanted something he went for it and if he had to he would break the law to do so. And yet somewhere there was a wrong note. Abby searched around in her mind, trying to find what it was, and then she remembered the pleasure with which people had greeted him at his old college. Surely people who had known him so closely over a period of years would have realised what kind of man he was? Or perhaps something had made him turn bad after he had left college. The shock of his fiancée's death, perhaps?

Abby stole a glance in his direction. The red glow of his cigar vividly recalled the nights he had waited and watched outside her flat, and she shivered in sudden dread. No matter what he might have been once, Lance Lazenby was dangerous now. She stared blindly back at the dark ribbon of road unwinding beneath the headlights. The only real confusion was between her body and her mind; her mind knew that he was bad and she must reject him, but her body had been devastated by his arrant masculinity and rejection was the last thing it wanted.

CHAPTER FOUR

As they drove through London, getting ever nearer to the flat, so Abby's tension increased. She tried to talk herself out of it, telling herself that she had handled similar situations countless times before, that Lance was, after all, a gentleman, she only had to say no and he would go. But that idea only made her almost laugh aloud with irony—just as Lance would laugh if she tried it. The cassette player came to an end and Abby reached out rather desperately to turn it over. Lance had the same idea and their hands brushed. Abby gave a little gasp and jerked hers away as if it had been burned. He could hardly have failed to notice, but he only murmured an apology and turned the cassette.

Familiar landmarks appeared and Abby willed herself to keep cool, to think what the character she was playing would have done. She certainly wouldn't have let herself get into this state of fearful anticipation. Sitting back in her seat, she closed her eyes and tried to think herself into the part. She must be cool, sophisticated, not allow a situation to grow that she couldn't handle. The car stopped and Lance turned off the engine. Reluctantly Abby opened her eyes.

Lance smiled at her in the semi-darkness. 'Were you asleep?'

She shook her head. 'Not quite. But it's been such a full, interesting day.' She didn't say it, but left the implication that she was tired.

'Let me help you out.'

He came round to open the door for her and helped her to carry the gifts he had bought for her. As well as the tortoiseshell box, there was a pretty Wedgwood jasper ware powder bowl from Blenheim and some very expensive talc to put in it from a shop in Oxford. Abby unlocked the door of her flat and turned to take the things from him, but he pushed the door open for her with his free hand and stood waiting expectantly for her to go in ahead of him. And because he expected it, she did so, meekly walking into the flat and letting him shut the door behind them.

Lance put the parcels down and Abby tried to recover the situation. Smiling at him, she indicated the parcels and said lightly, 'I shall be spoilt.'

'Nonsense. Pretty girls should always be given presents. Let me help you with your jacket.'

'Thanks, but I think I'll keep it on until I've warmed up,' Abby said, although the central heating had kept the flat comfortably warm. She smiled at him again. 'It's been a most interesting day, thank you.'

'It was a pleasure,' Lance replied gravely, but with amusement beginning to show in his eyes.

'Do you often go back to your old college?'

'Not as often as I'd like to. I mostly go for reunion dinners and boat race night.'

'That sounds fun.' Still he didn't move to go, and Abby began to feel ridiculous, standing here in the hall. 'Would you like a drink before you go?' she asked, emphasising the end of the sentence.

'Thank you.'

He followed her into the sitting-room and Abby mixed the drinks, spilling the gin as she sloshed it haphazardly into the glasses. She gave him his glass and Lance raised it in a toast. 'To many more wonderful days like today.'

Somehow Abby managed a smile and Lance took a drink of his gin and his eyebrows went up. 'Do you mind if I put some more tonic in this; it's rather strong?'

'Oh, sorry. I wouldn't want you to get breathalysed on your *way home*.' She gave what she hoped was a casual laugh. She sat in the armchair as far away from the radiators as possible, feeling hot and uncomfortable in her woollen jacket. Feverishly she made conversation, finishing her drink and rather ostentatiously setting the empty glass down, hoping that Lance would take the hint, but he seemed in no hurry, nonchalantly taking his time over his drink, which now, admittedly, was rather a long one, and keeping up his end of the conversation. At last he put down his glass and stood up. Abby looked up at him with fast-beating heart, wishing he would go, afraid he wouldn't.

Reaching down, Lance took hold of her hands and pulled her to her feet. He didn't say anything, but his hands went to the buttons of her jacket, began to slowly undo them. Abby stared into his face, unable to move, as the jacket slipped from her shoulders and was tossed aside. Under it she wore a little matching waistcoat, and this, too, he undid and took off. Then he parted the collar of her silk blouse and slid a hand inside. 'Your skin is burning,' he said softly, his fingers caressing the column of her throat.

Abby tried to answer him, to give the light reply she would have used with any other man, that would keep the situation cool and manageable.

But somehow it wouldn't come out, she could only close her eyes and sigh as he undid the next two buttons of her blouse, then bent his dark head to kiss the valley between her breasts. 'Relax,' he murmured gently. 'You're as nervous as a cat.' Straightening up, he put his hands on her shoulders. 'What's the matter?'

She looked up at him, aware that he had given her a chance and all the possible excuses she could use flying through her head, but instead her hands went up to draw her blouse together and she said unsteadily, 'I—I don't want you to stay.'

A frown came into his eyes and her knuckles showed white as she gripped her blouse. 'Come and sit down.' He led her over to the settee and pulled her down beside him. 'Look, Abby, just because I insisted you give up Ross Newton it doesn't mean that I'm also going to insist on sleeping with you. The two don't necessarily go together, you know.'

'The-they don't?'

'No, they don't. You lovely little idiot!' He leant forward and kissed the tip of her nose. 'We have plenty of time to get to know each other. All the time in the world. I don't want to rush you into anything.' Abby's hands began to relax as she gazed at him in relief. But then he went on, 'I want you, of course I do—that goes without saying. You're far too lovely for me not to, and I hope that when we get to know each other better, you'll want it as well. But that's for the future. For now let's just concentrate on getting to know one another. Okay?'

'Okay,' Abby gave him a tremulous smile.

'Good.' He grinned suddenly and it was like coming face to face with a total stranger. 'Of course from my point of view the *sooner* we get to know each other the better.' His arm went round her. 'Now stop trembling. There's nothing to be afraid of. Nothing's going to happen until you want it to.'

Abby gazed at him, not quite believing what she was seeing or hearing. Where she had expected forcefulness she had found gentleness and consideration, and that grin had made him seem human for the first time since she had met him. Some of her reserve began to slip and she smiled back at him, overwhelmingly relieved that she was in no danger from him. And, perversely, now that she was out of danger, all she wanted was for him to kiss her. Moving closer to him, she leant against his shoulder. 'It's been a wonderful day,' she murmured.

'So it has. What shall we do tomorrow?'

'I don't mind. Whatever you like.'

'All right. Then we'll go and visit some friends of mine who have a place in Kent. I'll pick you up at ten.' He stood up. 'Now I'd better go before you start trembling again.'

She walked with him to the front door. Lance said goodnight and lifted a questioning eyebrow. With a little laugh, Abby went easily into his arms and let him kiss her, confident that she was safe. But within seconds desire flared through her veins and when he let her go she had to lean against the wall, her senses reeling.

Lance stared at her, his composure for once shaken. 'Make it soon, Abby,' he said unsteadily. 'Don't make me wait too long.'

The friends that Lance took her to turned out to live in a large and beautiful red-brick mansion built in the reign of Charles II. They approached the house through a long drive that wound through thin woodland and came upon it suddenly so that Abby caught her breath in surprise and wonder.

'Your friends live here?'

Lance drove up between twin lawns, one of which had been marked out as a putting green, the other as a croquet lawn, and drew up outside the main entrance. His friends, a married couple in their mid-thirties, plus their three children and several dogs, greeted them warmly and led them inside to what must once have been the great hall, wood-panelled and with two large fireplaces set into the far wall. After drinks, they had lunch in a circular dining-room that had been redecorated in the Georgian era with ornate plasterwork on the ceiling and around the doors and over the marble Adam fireplace. The windows overlooked the landscaped gardens and after lunch they went for a long walk around the grounds and saw the Italian garden, the wilderness where the children had a tree-house, and over to the stables where there was a horse or pony for each member of the family, according to size. Then they were taken on a tour of the house which seemed partly still in the seventeenth and eighteenth centuries and partly very much in the twentieth, because where once there had been coal and wine cellars down in the basement, there was now a large playroom with table-tennis and video games for the children, and a sauna and small gymnasium for the adults.

They left about seven, after late tea, and Lance drove unhurriedly back to London. He had his Rolls today and Abby was grateful for its roominess that put a large space between them.

'What did you think of the house?' Lance asked her.

'It's a beautiful place. And your friends seem so happy there. He was full of ideas for improving it, wasn't he?'

'Yes, but unfortunately he'll be unable to carry them out.'

'Oh?'

'He wants to sell.'

'That's a shame. I suppose it is a terribly expensive place to keep up.'

'It's partly that. Partly that his firm wants to open a New York office and it will mean him having to live in America for several years. He's tried finding someone to rent it, but no one wants to take it on for a short term. So he has to sell.' Lance paused, then said deliberately, 'Would you like to live in a place like that?'

'Good heavens, who wouldn't? It's a beautiful house. But what a responsibility!' Abby remembered that she was supposed to be stinking rich and looked at Lance in astonishment. 'You're not—you're not suggesting that I might want to buy it?'

He laughed. 'No, of course not. As a matter of fact I was thinking about buying it myself.'

'Oh!' That, coming on top of his earlier question, threw her completely. Lance glanced across at her and their eyes met. Amusement curved his lips at her confusion and Abby quickly looked away, colour heightening her cheeks.

He took her out every night during the next week, and she often saw him during the day as well; for lunch or for a quick visit to a saleroom. He phoned her, too, and always he brought or sent her presents: flowers, beautifully-embroidered handkerchiefs, small antiques, nothing too elaborate or expensive, but always in perfect taste. And every night when he brought her home he would kiss her goodnight and then leave, without trying to pressurise her in any way, although as the week progressed the kisses became longer and more passionate and Abby less and less able to resist.

Her mind and her body were constantly at war. If she hadn't been forewarned she could easily have fallen for Lance. She found him a stimulating companion, knowledgeable and witty, ready to teach if she wanted to learn and always listening to her opinions with attention and willing to debate if he didn't agree, not just push them aside as some men would have done. And he was very considerate, always making sure that she was comfortable and had everything she wanted, or what he thought she ought to want; like a taxi or car waiting the minute she stepped outside, the best seats at the opera, the best table in a restaurant, and courteous attention from waiters and the like at all times. Heady stuff, and if Abby hadn't often reminded herself that it was merely the background scenery to the part she was playing it would have gone to her head. It was certainly very easy to get used to.

But she was still restless in his company, still with her nerves stretched taut like wires whenever she was near him. She told herself that it was because she had to be constantly on her guard in case she made a mistake, and this was true to a certain extent, but in her heart she knew that it was because he had such a devastating impact on her sexually. He had only to touch her and she was filled with a fierce hunger to be loved, a need so intense that it left her scared and bewildered, never having experienced anything like it before. She had wanted men in the past, but never, never like this.

Charles Bradbury had told her to report to him as often as possible, but during that week she grew progressively reluctant to do so. The Lance that she knew and the one he had described to her just didn't seem to be the same person. But on the Friday evening, as she was getting ready to go out to dinner, he phoned. Thinking that it might be Lance, Abby answered the call.

'You haven't been in touch,' Bradbury said without preamble. 'Has anything gone wrong?'

'What? Oh no. It's just that we've been out every day; there hasn't been time.'

'Have you given him the pen yet?'

'No. There—er—hasn't been an opportunity.'

'Make one.' The order was peremptory and unlike his usual mild manner. 'I need hardly remind you, Miss Stevens, that I am not paying you to waste time. I have very largely deferred to your view on how to handle this matter, but now I must insist that you give him the pen as soon as possible. Do you understand?' Although Bradbury couched the request in far more reasonable terms it somehow seemed even more menacing.

'Yes, all right.'

That evening they went to the opera again, to see *Il Trovatore*, and afterwards dined and danced to the early hours. There was no question now that Lance wouldn't come into the flat. Abby sat on the settee with him, her head against his shoulder as they talked over the evening and discussed plans for the next day. But presently he turned her face towards him and kissed her, his mouth exploring hers, gently, sensuously. Abby sighed and moved closer into his embrace, her hands on his shoulders. His lips grew more insistent and she gave him what he wanted, opening her mouth to let him in.

'Abby. Oh, Abby, my darling!' His lips left her mouth to kiss her eyes, her throat, to bite the lobe of her ear so that she gasped and her fingers dug into him. He bore her back against the settee and pushed her dress off her shoulder so that he could kiss the long white column of her neck. Abby's hands moved in his hair; she wanted to urge his head downwards to her breasts, her body crying out for the touch of his lips, his hands. But somehow sanity intervened and she opened her eyes and sat up, pulling down the skirt of her dress which had ridden up almost to her hips.

Lance pushed a lock of hair off his forehead and straightened his tie, a rather rueful grin on his lips. He stood up. 'I'd better go before I forget all my good intentions. Which wouldn't be difficult,' he added, as Abby stood up beside him, her hair dishevelled, her green eyes soft and misty. 'God, you're beautiful,' he said unsteadily. 'There's so much I . . .' He stopped abruptly.

'What were you going to say?' Abby put her arms round his waist and leant against him.

'It doesn't matter. Now isn't the time.' He buried his face in her hair for a moment and then stood back. 'I must go.' He went to do up his jacket, felt something in an inside pocket. 'I almost forgot.' He took out a small jeweller's box and handed it to her. 'To add to your collection,' he said lightly.

Inside the box was a brooch; an exquisitely worked cameo depicting the head of a man and set around with pearls.

'Oh, Lance, it's—it's perfect! Who is it?'

'I have it on good authority that it's Napoleon. There's every reason to believe that the brooch was made for the Empress Marie Louise.'

Abby looked at the lovely jewel in her hand, marvelling at the delicate workmanship and genuinely thrilled by its history. To own something that Napoleon himself might have touched, that had been worn by an Empress! Her artistic and imaginative soul delighted in those things, while her practical side told her it must have cost the earth. Impulsively she reached up and kissed him. 'I shall treasure it always. I can't thank you enough. It's beautiful!'

He smiled, pleased by her enthusiasm. 'It's nothing. Think of me sometimes when you wear it.'

He turned to go, but Abby caught his arm, realising that this was the perfect opportunity. 'You're always giving me presents, so I got one for you.' She crossed to the antique writing desk and took out the pen which she had wrapped in gilt paper with a matching bow. 'Here.' She handed it to him with a smile, almost forgetting what it contained.

Lance took it rather slowly, his eyes on her face. He took off the paper and opened the case, stood looking down at the pen for a long moment.

'I had your initials put on it,' Abby said, suddenly nervous now. 'I hope you like it.'

He seemed to have to pull himself together, as if he'd been miles away. 'Yes, of course. Thank you.'

'You'll use it?' She moved nearer, looking at him uncertainly, expecting him to have shown more pleasure.

'Every day.' He slipped the pen into his inside pocket and smiled at her, but there was a bleakness in his eyes that she didn't understand. Picking up the case he put that, too, in his jacket pocket, and then left, after affirming their arrangements for the next day.

Abby watched him go with puzzled eyes, wondering what she had done wrong, whether she had made him suspicious at all. Or perhaps it just wasn't the done thing in his circle for women to give presents in return. Perhaps it put him on a par with a gigolo or something—they were always rewarded for their services with gold cigarette cases, could it be that the modern equivalent was gold pens with their initials and inset with LCD digital clocks? The thought made her giggle uneasily. Then she looked at the brooch he had given her. It was a lovely thing and she would enjoy having it in her possession for a short time, but when this was all over it would, of course, go back to Lance along with all the other things he'd given her. Abby pushed that thought away, into the future.

Well, at least she had planted the pen, which should keep Charles Bradbury off her back for a while. And perhaps she had only imagined that slight change in Lance, she told herself reassuringly. Nevertheless, she lay awake for a long time that night, the doubt nagging at her mind.

The next morning, she phoned Bradbury first thing and told him the good news. She had hardly put the phone down before a man who introduced himself as Mr Lazenby's secretary rang to say that Lance had been called away unexpectedly to a business meeting and wouldn't be able to meet her at all that day.

Had he realised that something was wrong? Had he guessed and found the bug? Abby worried about it all day; toyed with the idea of phoning Charles Bradbury again, then changed her mind. But at nine-thirty that night all her fears were laid to rest when Lance phoned, sounding the same as ever, apologising for having to break their date but explaining that he had had to fly up to Edinburgh and had only just got back.

'We'll swop Saturday for Sunday, shall we?' he asked. 'I'll come over at ten as we planned?'

'That's fine. I'll look forward to seeing you. 'Bye, Lance.'

'Goodnight, darling.'

Strange, Abby thought inconsequentially as she put down the phone, he called her darling often, and yet she had never used that term to him. In show business everyone called everyone else darling, whether male or female, and it rolled off the tongue without thinking, but something had made her baulk at using endearments with Lance. That night she slept well, glad that her worries had come to nothing, and was waiting with a smile when he came the next day.

He had brought a polaroid camera with him and they took several shots of the Lucrezia Borgia bracelet, then spent an interesting day in the National Portrait Gallery and the British Museum trying to find evidence that it had really belonged to that infamous lady. They got sidetracked often, and they didn't dig up anything, but it was still a very enjoyable day. And Abby had the satisfaction of seeing Lance take the pen from his pocket and use it several times. At least, she supposed that it was satisfaction she felt.

During the next week, she saw Lance as often as before. Once he was delayed and asked her to meet him at his office. Abby took a taxi into the City and it pulled up outside a big old stone building just off Threadneedle Street where the Bank of England is situated. She expected him to have just a suite of offices, but it turned out from the name-plates on the wall at the entrance that his holding company and its subsidiaries occupied the whole building. Abby pushed open the swing doors and found herself in a large and pleasant reception area. It was seven o'clock and the staff had gone, but a uniformed security man immediately came towards her. 'Miss Stevens?'

'Yes, that's right.'

'Mr Lazenby told us you were coming. If you'll come with me, miss, I'll take you up to his office.'

There was a lift that took them up to the fifth floor, and then Abby followed him down a carpeted corridor to a door marked with Lance's name. The man knocked and opened the door for her, but the room was empty.

'He must still be in conference. If you'll wait here, miss, I'll fetch him for you.'

'Thank you.' Abby walked into the room and looked around with interest, realising that this was a golden opportunity to find out Lance's business secrets; or it would be if she only knew what to look for. But perhaps there was something she could do. Switching on her little cassette recorder, one eye always on the door, she quickly went through the small pile of papers and letters in Lance's tray, reading off the names of companies and people wherever they were mentioned. Then she went through some files on his desk, listing their subjects. She had almost finished when she heard voices in the corridor outside, so she hastily straightened the files and moved towards the window, pretending to be looking out as Lance entered the room followed by two other men.

'Sorry to have kept you waiting, darling. It was unavoidable, I'm afraid.' He came over and kissed her, then drew her forward. 'Darling, I'd like you to meet two of my co-directors. This is Bill Faden, the Company Secretary, and this is Anthony Oliver, our Financial Director.'

'How do you do?' She shook hands with the two men and they smiled in return, but they seemed rather stiff and unnatural, their eyes concentrating on her face. Abby looked at Lance rather questioningly and he laughed, putting his arm round her waist.

'You'll have to forgive these two staring at you, Abby. They're not used to seeing such beautiful girls around the place.'

Bill Faden grinned. 'That's true. And you don't usually bring your . . . that is, you've never before . . .' He groaned as he realised he was only getting in a deeper mess. 'Trust me to put my big foot in it!'

'Both feet,' Lance told him with derisive good humour. 'I just have to put these papers in the safe and then we can go.' To Abby's surprise he went to one of the filing cabinets, pressed a switch on the inside of the top drawer, and part of the wall slid to one side revealing a steel door. Lance said his name and a section of the door clicked and revealed a sort of small screen. Lance put his hand flat on the screen, held it there for a moment, then the door slid noiselessly open. Behind the door was a walk-in safe as long as a small room.

'Good heavens!' Abby exclaimed. 'How ingenious! I'd never have known it was there.'

'Nor, we hope, will any burglars who break in,' Bill Faden said drily.

'They shouldn't, not with all this technology.' Lance put the files from his desk into the safe and then closed the door. 'You see, it's worked by a computer which is programmed to open the door only when it recognises the voice and handprint of certain members of the staff,' he explained.

'It certainly makes ordinary safes look extremely old-fashioned!'

'This is a technological age,' Lance said lightly, his eyes going over her approvingly. Abby was wearing a very simply-cut blue dress, its only ornament the cameo brooch he had given her at the neck. He turned to the other men. 'Sorry to keep you so late. Perhaps you'll let me have any further ideas on what we discussed in the morning.'

Recognising that they were being dismissed, the men shook hands with Abby and left. Lance saw them to the door and then turned to her. 'Come here,' he said softly.

Abby gazed into his face for a long moment, then walked across the room and into his arms, forgetting the role she was playing, forgetting everything but the need to be near him. He kissed her expertly, holding her against him, moulding her body against his. 'Do you really want to go to that concert tonight?' he asked her, his mouth against her throat.

'Why? Do you want to go somewhere else?'

'You haven't seen my flat yet. I thought we could have dinner and then go back there—listen to some music.'

An inner voice warned her that it could be dangerous, that she was playing with fire, but his

hands were on her hips, pulling her against the
taut hardness of his body. 'All right.' She
murmured the words unsteadily, her breath catching
in her throat.

'Darling!' Triumph came into Lance's grey eyes
as he kissed her again.

They had dinner in an intimate little Italian
trattoria in the West End, with red and white
checked tableclothes, where Italian music played in
the background, and where they ate pasta in rich
sauces and drank wine from bottles covered round
with woven straw. They sat in a booth, opposite
one another, and whenever their knees or hands
happened to touch Abby experienced a kind of
electric shock of anticipation that made her unable
to eat. Afterwards, while they waited for their
coffee to be served, Lance reached across the table
and took her hand, held it between his. 'What do
you think of the restaurant?' he asked softly.

'It's great. Just like being in Italy.'

'Have you been there before?'

'No.' Abby shook her head. 'But I'd love to go.
I . . .' She stopped, her voice trailing away
uncertainly. Was it her imagination, or had
Lance's hands jerked just then?

But he was smiling at her quite matter-of-factly.
'I'm glad you've enjoyed it. We must come here
again some time.' He glanced down at her hands.
'You don't wear any rings.'

She shrugged lightly. 'Nobody ever gave me
one.'

Lance was about to say something, but the
waiter arrived with their coffee and he had to let
go her hand. 'Would you like a liqueur?'

She declined, knowing that she had already had
enough to drink, not that she'd needed it; she was

on a high before they'd even entered the restaurant. Lance didn't hurry over his coffee, lighting one of his thin black cigars and telling her about a book he had been reading, and from there they somehow got on to the Great Wall of China and then to Chinese porcelain. They left about ten, and Lance drove skilfully through the maze of traffic up to Hyde Park Corner, turning in through the gates and driving through the Park past the dark waters of the Serpentine, to leave by another gate and pull up outside a block of flats close by.

His flat was on the sixth floor and made her own look poky by comparison. It was very masculine, with black leather chesterfields and lots of book shelves and glass-fronted cabinets displaying his collection of silver. There was also a large TV set, a music centre with quadraphonic sound and all the usual amplifiers and tuners, as well as one of the new laser disc players.

Lance poured her a drink from a well-stocked bar built into the corner and brought it over to her.

'Nice little place you've got here,' Abby said flippantly.

He gave a mock leer. 'All the better for luring innocent maidens into my lair.'

She opened her eyes wide, immediately joining in the game. 'Oh, sir, pray don't harm me! Take all my money, but let me go.'

He laughed evilly. 'It isn't your money I want.'

'Oh, I'm so afraid!'

Lance laughed, but then his face became serious. 'Are you—still afraid?'

She looked at him, then down at the drink in her hands. 'Yes, I . . . I don't know.'

He stood looking down at her bent head for a

moment, then moved away. 'I'll put some music on.'

Expecting something classical, Abby was agreeably surprised when he selected a James Last record. 'Let's dance,' he said.

Abby kicked off her shoes, which brought her down a good three inches, about level with his shoulder, and they danced to some fast beat numbers, but then he changed the record and the music became slow and smoochy. He wore an aftershave lotion that had the insinuating tang of musk. Abby remembered reading in a women's magazine that musk was the biggest turn-on that had ever been found, and she wondered why he wore it; he certainly didn't need to add fuel to the fire. Because already desire was burning through her veins, making her body ache with need.

'Abby.' Lance stopped dancing and drew her very close, his mouth seeking hers. There was a hardness in his kiss tonight; it reminded her of the way he had kissed her that first time at her flat, but since then he'd been gentler with her, tender almost. But now his lips were fierce again, taking instead of sharing, asserting his masculine strength so that her body arched against his. His hands went to her hair, pulling it almost roughly free of its restraining clips, and then he wound his hands in it, used it to hold her head still as his mouth ravaged hers.

'Oh, God!' Abby's lips parted under his onslaught, her arms went round his neck and she clung to him, the hardness of his body rousing her to fever pitch so that she kissed him passionately in return.

Lance stooped and picked her up, carried her over to one of the chesterfields and laid her down, her head on a cushion. His hands went to her dress, began to undo the buttons, unpinned the brooch and tossed it to one side.

'Lance.' Her hands came up to cover his in a feeble attempt to stop him, but he pushed them impatiently aside, and then her dress was off her shoulders, her bra undone and his hands on her breasts. Abby gasped, feeling herself harden under his fingers. He touched her expertly, knowing exactly how to rouse her. She moved against his hands, loving what he was doing, wanting him to go on for ever. A shuddering moan broke from her as his fingers squeezed, hurt a little. Opening her eyes, she found him looking down at her, a strange almost dispassionate look on his face.

He saw her eyes were open and said, 'You're very beautiful,' in a tone that made it not a compliment but a statement. Leaning forward, he began to kiss her breasts, driving her crazy so that she groaned and moved against him, her hands in his hair, holding him there. But then his hands were on her dress again, pulling it down, and she let him go so that he could take it off. Under it she was wearing only lacy black pants and a black suspender belt to hold up her stockings.

Lance's jaw tightened as he looked down at her. His hands moved caressingly down her waist and hips, slid under the edge of her pants. 'Are you still afraid?' His voice was harsh, unsteady.

Abby stared into his set face, remembering all the warnings she had been given about him. But beside the yearning hunger he aroused in her betraying body, with his hands on her, delighting her, it didn't matter. It was insignificant. All that mattered was that they were a man and a woman who wanted and needed the fulfilment only each other's bodies could give. 'No,' she answered softly, 'I'm not afraid any more.'

Once more a flicker of triumph shone in his eyes. He kissed her again and Abby returned it passionately, eager now for him to make love to her. But, amazingly, he suddenly broke away and got to his feet. 'I'm sorry.' He walked over to the bar and began to pour himself a drink, standing with his back to her. 'I have no right to force myself on you. You trusted me when you came here, and I should have respected that. But you're so lovely that . . .' He broke off and took a long swallow of his drink.

Abby stared at him. Nothing like this had ever happened to her before. She didn't know whether to laugh or cry. 'Really, Lance, I . . .'

But he interrupted her. 'Get dressed, Abby. I'll take you home.'

Slowly she sat up and fumbled her way into her dress, bewildered by the transition from passion back to normality. She found her shoes and put them on, then looked round unseeingly. 'My—my brooch.'

'Here.' Lance finished his drink and picked the brooch up from the small table on which he had tossed it. 'Let me put it on for you.'

He fastened it on, his fingers brushing her breasts as he did so, so that she trembled convulsively. He must have felt it, but strangely she saw only irony in his face. Then it was quickly gone as she said uncertainly, 'Lance, I . . .'

'Hush.' He put his finger on her lips. 'All I want you to say is that you forgive me. I could have spoilt something very wonderful.'

As far as Abby was concerned, he already had. She had never felt so empty or frustrated in her life. And she just couldn't understand it. She would have been willing to bet every penny she had that Lance wasn't the kind of man to back down in a situation like that, whatever scruples he might have. She had as good as told him to go ahead anyway, so what more did he need? And as for all that about forcing himself on her and putting her trust in him—it was just way out of character. 'I don't understand,' she burst out.

Moving his hands to her shoulders, he said earnestly, 'Darling, we haven't known each other long and maybe this is too soon to say it, but—you're very, very special. And I don't want anything to cheapen or spoil what we have going for us. Now do you understand?'

Abby nodded slowly, gazing at him open-mouthed. She understood all right; he was falling in love with her. The rich seducer she had been sent to help bring to justice was actually falling in love with her! It was such an incredible thing to happen that it was almost funny. Or at least it would be if she didn't feel so crazily mixed up inside.

CHAPTER FIVE

CHARLES Bradbury was absolutely jubilant when Abby told him that she had actually been into Lance's office, and even more so when he learnt that she had also been into his flat. He made her get a taxi at once and join him at a small pub in the Mile End Road where they sat in a discreet corner and he made her go over everything she had seen so many times that she got annoyed. 'I've already told you it all at least four times; surely you don't need me to tell you again.'

'Are you sure that's all he did—just said his name and put his hand on the door-plate? He didn't punch any numbers or anything?'

'No, that's all he did once the panel in the wall had slid back. But why do you want to know about the safe? You said you didn't intend to break in or do anything like that. You're not planning another Watergate, are you?' Abby asked, only half jokingly.

Bradbury laughed. 'No, of course not. I was just interested, that's all. It sounds the kind of thing we could use in my own business.' He patted her hand in pleasure. 'You've done marvellously well. I'll go through this tape and with any luck it might give us a clue to what Lazenby is planning. If we can prove he's been share-juggling, we'll have him.'

'We?'

'Sarah and I; the companies he's broken on the way up; the shareholders he's ruined. I'm not the only one who wants to see justice done, Abigail.

It's just that I'm in a better position than anyone else to do it.'

It was the first time he had used her Christian name; he must be very pleased. She smiled, glad that she had been of some practical help at last. Not that she had told him everything about last night; he had only got the expurgated version. Somehow she just hadn't been able to bring herself to tell him of the near certainty that Lance was falling in love with her. He could have used it to his advantage, she supposed, but somehow that just wasn't the kind of weapon you used on a man, no matter what he had done. Luckily Bradbury hadn't asked any questions about what had happened at the flat; he'd been too elated with the knowledge of her being there.

'Now that you've been to his office and his home, there'll be no difficulty in your going there again. And you'll be able to plant some more bugs,' he said excitedly. 'Look, I've brought some for you. You just have to peel this little piece of paper off the back and then you stick them where they won't be noticed: under his desk, behind pictures—oh, and definitely in his telephones.'

'Telephones?'

'Yes, at his office and at his flat.'

'But I don't know how to fix them,' Abby objected.

'It's really very simple. All you have to do is to unscrew the mouthpiece of the receiver, slip the bug into the works and screw it up again. A child could do it. Practise on your own phone if you're at all doubtful. Now, what bills have you for me?'

Abby handed them over and he gave her a cheque, not only to cover them and for more petty cash, but also because he was so pleased, a thousand pounds of the money he had promised her when the job was done.

'If–if that tape gives you the information you want—will that be the end of it?' Abby asked slowly.

Mr Bradbury's eyebrows rose over the top of his glasses, making him look like a clown. 'Is there some reason for you asking that?'

'It's just that it's becoming rather a strain having to be on my guard the whole time. I didn't expect I would be seeing so much of him, that I'd get a chance to switch off every now and again, but I'm seeing him every day now.'

'Are you saying you want more money?' he asked drily.

Abby flushed and said shortly, 'No, I'm not. I'm just asking you to—to get this over with as soon as you can, that's all.'

'Which is also what I want. But just how quickly we can achieve our ends rather depends on how quickly and how well you plant those bugs, doesn't it?'

'Haven't you learnt anything useful from the pen bug?' she asked.

He frowned. 'Unfortunately, no. A lot of what came through was so muffled it was indecipherable, and what has been clear has been just ordinary business talk. But I'm still hoping, of course. But once you've planted those bugs we should be able to get the information we want very quickly.'

'What will happen to him—to Lazenby?' Abby asked, her voice suddenly sticking in her throat.

Bradbury shot her a quick glance and then shrugged. 'I can't say exactly. The police may or may not decide to prosecute him for fraud, depending on how much evidence there is. But whatever happens his reputation in the City will be ruined. He'll be shown up for the liar and cheat that he is. But even that wouldn't make up for what he did to my daughter—nothing can give back what he did to her.' His voice broke and he took off his glasses and rubbed them vigorously.

'No, of course not,' Abby agreed. She picked up her bag. 'I'll plant the bugs as soon as I have an opportunity.'

They left the pub separately and she took a taxi back to her flat. She had intended to do some odd jobs and then go shopping, but she felt strangely restless, unable to concentrate on anything, feeling suddenly desperately tired of this role she was playing. On impulse, she changed into a pair of jeans and a baggy sweater, tied her hair into a simple ponytail and ran out of the flat, catching a bus on the corner that went past her old flat in Clapham. She didn't have a key any more, having let someone else take over her share of the flat on the understanding that she could move back in again whenever she wanted to. At first she thought that there was no one in, but when she had held her finger on the bell for a second time, the door opened and Liz poked her head out, her blonde hair tousled and traces of make-up on her face.

'Oh, hi, Abby.' She opened the door and yawned heavily. She was wearing only a short, bright red nightshirt with the words 'Yale University' on the front. 'Come on in.'

'Were you still in bed?' Abby asked.

'Mm. We had quite a night last night. It was someone's birthday and the party went on till about eight this morning.' Liz slumped down into a chair at the kitchen table. 'Make me a coffee, will you? I've got a splitting headache.'

'You mean a hangover, don't you?'

'No, I think it was the noise of the disco; I can still hear it going on in my head.'

Abby laughed and put the kettle on. The sink was piled with dirty crockery and the kitchen was very untidy. In fact the whole flat looked pretty grotty, as if it hadn't been properly cleaned for weeks; since she'd left it, in fact. It also seemed terribly small and cramped after the flat in Chelsea. They sat over their mugs of coffee, talking shop, Liz telling who had got what job and who hadn't. It was a world with which Abby was completely familiar and she had expected to drop back into it as easily and comfortably as putting on her jeans and sweater, but she felt oddly detached from it, as though she wasn't a part of it any more. Which was ridiculous, when she had only been away for a month or so. She tried to concentrate, to get back into the show-business atmosphere—she needed to, desperately. But it just wasn't there any more.

As soon as she could, Abby made an excuse and left, glad to be out in the open again away from the stuffy, unkempt atmosphere of her old home. It wasn't too far back to Chelsea and she decided to walk, trying to sort out the confusion in her mind. The shops she passed were full of the new summer fashions and ordinarily she would have been drawn irresistibly, but today she walked with brooding steps, unaware of her surroundings. She hadn't slept much after Lance had brought her home last night, had lain awake trying to still the frustrated yearning that was like a physical pain, trying to convince herself that she was lucky that she had been given a way out, that Lance was no good to her or to any woman. But nothing had been any good and she tossed restlessly in bed, her fingers digging into the pillow as her hot body cried out for his touch, his love.

Now she sighed as she walked along, wishing she had never got involved in all this, wishing it was all over and done with. Nothing seemed the same any more; she was becoming too used to the rich life, she supposed. It would be hard to go back, to be just Abby Stevens, struggling actress, again, but the sooner she could the better for her. And it would be hard to be unattached again, with no man perpetually taking her out, phoning, sending flowers. No man whose touch could set her nerves tingling, whose kiss could make her feel wanton with desire. She turned into the small square opposite her block of flats and walked along abstractedly, tall, slender and graceful as a willow, her chestnut hair swinging and shining like polished copper in the sun. She crossed the quiet tree-lined road and strode across the courtyard, then stopped precipitately, her heart lurching. There was a silver Rolls parked outside the entrance and Lance was leaning against it, smoking a cigarette.

When he saw her, he straightened up slowly, throwing the cigarette away. His expression was one of surprise, and Abby realised that he hadn't recognised her at first because she was out of character. He had never before seen her in casual gear. For a long moment neither of them moved, then Abby began to walk slowly towards him. Lance waited for her to come to him, his grey eyes fixed on her intently. She felt at a loss; this wasn't the right costume for her part and the ad lib dialogue wouldn't come. Even when she came right up to him she couldn't find any words to say.

There was a strange, almost bitter look on Lance's face, a look that frightened her a little, although she didn't know why. Suddenly he reached out and caught her arm, pulled her roughly to him and kissed her, one hand on each side of her head. His kiss, too, was rough, almost as if he was enjoying hurting her. Tears pricked at her eyes, but not of pain. She wanted to kiss him back just as fiercely, but his mouth dominated and she could only submit to a will that was far stronger than her own. At last he lifted his head, but he still kept his hands on either side of her face. 'That was for me,' he said, in a voice that was almost a snarl. Then he let her go and stepped back abruptly.

Abby didn't try to work it out, she just stood there staring at him, feeling strangely cold inside, a chill in her veins as she saw the harshness in his face. But then there was the sound of a car hooter behind them and Lance blinked, his manner changing completely.

After glancing round, he put a hand under Abby's elbow and drew her to one side. 'We seem to be blocking the way—and we appear to have acquired an audience.'

A car moved past them, the driver with a big grin on his face. And when Abby looked she saw a group of several residents standing on the steps, watching them with expressions ranging from amusement to disgust.

'Let's go in, shall we?' With his hand still on her arm, Lance led her towards the entrance, giving the people there such an arrogant look that they hastily went about their business.

Still feeling somewhat bemused, Abby let him take control. She was trying to work out how she could explain the clothes she was wearing, but her mind kept going back to that kiss. He had seemed so different, almost as if he was kissing her against his will; she was sure he hadn't intended to, not with all those people around. Strangely for him, he'd lost his cool and had acted completely outside his character. And afterwards, when he said, 'That was for me'; that was strange, too.

She thought he might say something to explain his behaviour when they got in the flat, but he didn't. He merely turned and ran his eyes over her, raising his brows questioningly so that Abby felt compelled to give *him* an explanation. 'I went for a walk on Hampstead Heath,' she told him.

'What's wrong with the local parks?'

'They're too landscaped and formal. I wanted somewhere more open and—natural.'

Lance smiled slightly and crossed to take hold of her hands. 'You felt you wanted to commune with nature?'

'Something like that,' Abby agreed lightly. Then, before they could get on to dangerous ground, 'I hope you weren't waiting too long. I didn't expect to see you this afternoon.'

'No, I was only there for about ten minutes.' Letting go of her hands, he moved over to a chair and sat down. 'I brought you the catalogue for the jewellery sale at Christie's next week. There's a necklace that once belonged to Sarah Bernhardt in their list. I thought you might like to go along and see it.'

'Is it already on view?'

'No, but I've telephoned one of the directors who's a friend of mine. He'll let us see it privately, if you're interested.'

'Of course. Do you mean now?' she asked nervously.

Lance nodded. 'That was the general idea.'

'I'll have to change. Shall I meet you there?'

'Why don't I wait for you? I haven't got any appointments this afternoon.'

There was nothing she could do but agree, of course, although she felt oddly reluctant to have him in the flat while she changed her clothes. Which on the surface of it was silly—until she remembered that kiss. And he'd given no word of explanation for it, nothing. And somehow she didn't have the nerve to ask.

She changed as quickly as she could, assuming the part she was playing as she assumed the couturier clothes. She added make-up, put her hair up and covered it with an elegant hat with little feathers that curved down one side of her face. Her Gucci bag and matching gloves, and she was ready to step on the stage again.

Lance was standing looking out of the window, smoking a cigarette. He turned and ran his eyes over her, but his expression was far different from when he had watched her in her jeans just a short while ago. Now his face showed only what she expected to see: approval and admiration. The large, squashy bag she had been carrying then was still on the coffee table where she had dropped it when she came in. Abby went to it to get her purse; the bugs Bradbury had given her caught her eye and she quickly picked up a few of them without letting Lance see and slipped them with the purse into her other handbag.

She turned to smile at him. 'I'm sorry to have kept you waiting so long.'

'On the contrary,' he smiled in return, 'you've been amazingly quick. I know of no other female who's managed to change in such a short time.'

Which left Abby wondering just how many

women he had known well enough to wait around for while they changed.

The necklace, which they were discreetly shown in a back room at the auction house, was beautiful. Made in the shape of a snake, it circled round the neck in a coil of gold inlaid with small rubies and emeralds, the head forming a pendant of cut opals with two larger rubies for the eyes. It was in the art nouveau style and had been specially made for the great Sarah Bernhardt to wear in the role of Cleopatra. It was a thing of interest and beauty in itself, but to Abby it was doubly so because of its connection with one of the greatest women of her own profession. Not that she admitted that to Lance, of course; she merely exclaimed, admired and asked all the right questions.

'Will you bid for it?' Lance asked her as they left the auctioneers.

'I shall certainly try. How much do you think it will go for?'

'I'm no expert on jewellery, I'm afraid. I'd guess between fifteen and twenty thousand.'

Abby nodded, thinking she could always pretend to bid for it and then back down. She would have to talk to Charles Bradbury, see what he advised.

Afterwards they went to see a new exhibition of paintings that had opened a couple of days before at the Royal Academy. Abby knew very little about art and thought it safe to say so, but Lance, as always, was knowledgeable on the subject and quite happy to teach her.

Glancing at his watch as they left the Academy, he said, 'Shall we go to the concert we missed last night?' and when she agreed, went on, 'In that case we have a couple of hours to kill. There doesn't seem to be much point in splitting up, so why don't you come back to my flat with me while *I* change? We could have a drink there and a meal after the concert.'

Lance took rather longer to change than Abby had. It gave her ample time to take advantage of the opportunity he had given her and plant several of the bugging devices: one in his telephone, one under the coffee table in his sitting-room, and two in his study. There was even time for her to pour herself a second drink and try to calm her jangling nerves a little before he came back into the room, but even so he took her by surprise so that she started and spilt some of her drink when she turned and saw him.

'Oh! You made me jump,' she said unnecessarily.

Lance smiled lazily. 'You must have a guilty conscience.' He put a hand lightly on her arm. 'Why, you're trembling. Is something the matter?'

There was nothing but concern in his face and voice, but even so Abby still felt a cold rush of fear. 'No, of course not,' she answered, trying to pass it off as lightly as she could. 'It was just a cold shiver. Perhaps someone walked over my grave.'

'You poor darling! Are you sure you want to go to the concert?' He put his hands on her shoulders and began to gently massage them, his touch immediately sending sensuous messages running through her veins.

'Yes, of course. We missed it last night, remember?' The moment the words were out Abby wished them unsaid. This wasn't the time or place to remember last night; it could so easily happen again but with far different consequences.

'How could I forget?' Lance murmured, his lips against her ear, moving slowly, sensuously along the line of her neck, her throat, driving her crazy with longing to feel his lips on her mouth. She closed her eyes, her breath uneven, lips parted, waiting for his kiss.

But to her surprise and disappointment, Lance straightened up and said thickly, 'Maybe we'd better go. Missing that concert could well become a habit.'

Abby opened her eyes in surprise and caught him looking at her with a bleakly sardonic twist to his mouth, but this was quickly gone as he smiled ruefully. She smiled uncertainly in reply and turned to get her jacket.

They left shortly afterwards, taking the lift down to the ground floor, but as they were about to leave the building, Lance gave an exclamation of annoyance. 'I've left my car keys behind. Sorry, darling, I won't be more than a minute.'

But Abby was chatting to the man on duty in the lobby for several minutes before he came back, apologising again, and hurrying her out to the car.

That she would have a similar fortunate opportunity to plant the rest of the bugs in Lance's office was too much to hope for, and she had started to rack her brains to think up an excuse for calling on him there, when again fate played into her hands. They were in the Rolls one afternoon only a few days later, when the telephone began to bleep. Lance answered it with growing annoyance, then put down the receiver and turned to her apologetically.

'I'm sorry, darling, but I'm afraid I have to go to the office. Some sort of crisis.'

'Which they can't handle without you?' Abby allowed disappointment to show in her voice.

Lance shook his head and gave a short laugh. 'It appears not. Would you like me to drop you at Harrods or somewhere and then come back for you?'

Abby pretended to consider the question for a few seconds, then shook her head with a smile. 'No, I'd rather wait for you.'

'Darling.' He picked up her hand, twining her fingers in his, then lifted it to his mouth and kissed each of her fingers in turn, his eyes warm.

Back at his office, he ensconced her in a comfortable chair, found her some magazines to look at, and instructed his secretary's assistant—a female this time—to bring her some coffee. Then he hurried away to settle the problems that had cropped up. The coffee was brought to her in delicate china on a silver tray. It made Abby think of all the hundreds of weak, muddy-looking coffees she'd drunk out of plastic cups from vending machines at rehearsal or audition halls, and she grimaced at the memory.

'Is there something wrong with the coffee, Miss Stevens?' the secretary asked anxiously.

'Oh, no.' Abby looked at the woman, who was quite a bit older than herself, and smiled. 'It's perfect. I'm afraid I was thinking of something else entirely.'

'I see.' The woman was in no hurry to go. She was running her eyes over Abby critically from head to toe, taking in everything she was wearing and probably pricing it to the nearest pound as well. It had created quite a stir when Lance had escorted her into the building. When she had visited it before all the staff had gone home, but now it was full of people, waiting for lifts, walking along the corridors, and all who had seen her with

Lance had had a good look, some discreetly, some quite openly, as now. 'Is there anything else I can get you? I'm afraid we don't often have ladies visiting the office,' she added with a nervous laugh.

'No, thank you,' Abby answered firmly, wanting her out of the way. 'Lance—Mr Lazenby left me something to read.' She indicated the magazines and dismissively picked one up.

'Oh, well ...' The woman hovered for a moment longer, obviously longing to chat, but Abby lowered her head and opened the magazine so that she had no choice but to go. 'Do ring if you want anything, won't you?'

'Yes. Thank you.' Abby nodded and turned back to her magazine.

As the woman closed the door behind her the thought flashed through Abby's mind that it would now go round the whole firm that Lance's girl-friend was a stuck-up snob who thought herself too good to even talk to his employees. But this was instantly pushed aside as she dropped the magazine and stood up, grabbing her bag and searching for the bugs. Nervously she hurried over to the phone and picked up the receiver, her fingers slippery with fear so that she fumbled as she tried to unscrew it, her eyes on the door in case Lance came in and caught her. Suddenly she almost dropped the receiver in fright as a voice said, 'Can I help you?'

For a full minute Abby was too petrified to think, and the voice repeated the question, puzzlement in the tone now. Of course—it was the operator. She should have realised that all the phones in the building were connected to a switchboard.

'Could—could I have an outside line, please?'

Somehow Abby managed to think coherently again. The familiar soft note of the dialling tone came through and she hurriedly went on with her task and fixed the bug in place. Then it occurred to her that the operator might be listening in, so she had better make an actual call, so she phoned her hairdresser and pretended to check the time of her next appointment. This done, she fixed a bug under Lance's desk and another behind one of the paintings on the far wall. There were only two left now.

One of the doors opening out of Lance's office led straight into the director's boardroom. Abby crossed to it and gently opened the door an inch. The boardroom with its long highly-polished table set round with a dozen identical chairs, was empty. She tiptoed in and attached a bug under the top end of the table where a portrait of an elderly man who looked remarkably like Lance was hung on the wall. Then she crept down to the other end to fix the second bug, the eyes in the portrait seeming to follow her relentlessly all the way. She had just put her hand under the table and was pressing the bug into place when there was the sound of a raised voice behind her. She froze with fear, the hairs on the back of her neck standing on end. Slowly she turned her head, but there was no one there. Then the voice came again, and she saw that another door was open a little and gave on to what must be the director's dining-room where two women were clearing up after lunch. Abby rammed the bug into place and fled back to Lance's office, almost collapsing into the chair, and shaking with reaction. Thank God that now it would soon be over, that she'd done all that Charles Bradbury had asked of her. Now that the bugs were planted he would soon get all the information he wanted and she would be free again. Hands trembling with emotion, she tried to pick up the coffee cup, but the liquid tipped crazily, spilling the coffee into the saucer. Stupidly it made her want to cry and she set the cup down angrily. He deserved it, didn't he? Deserved everything that was coming to him. Prison, public ridicule, the scorn and contempt of everyone who knew him. He had behaved cruelly to the innocent and deserved to be treated cruelly and ruthlessly in return. There could be nothing but good in bringing such a man to justice. So why did she feel so bad, so guilty, as if she wanted to die?

It was a good twenty minutes later before Lance rejoined her, and by then she was outwardly calm again, idly leafing through a magazine.

'Have you been terribly bored?'

'No, of course not.' Abby put the magazine aside and smiled at him. 'Your secretary looked after me very well. Have you sorted out your problems?'

'As far as I can. We're contemplating a take-over, but a few snags have cropped up. But I mustn't bore you with business worries.'

'I'm afraid I know little about business, but I really feel I ought to learn. Ought I to buy some shares in this firm you're going to take over?'

Lance burst out laughing. 'It would be most unethical of me to tell you that.'

'Would it?' Abby wrinkled her brow. 'Why?'

He laughed again. 'I can see I have a great deal to teach you about the stock market. You're not allowed to give inside information so that your friends can make a killing.'

Abby moved close to him and put her arms

round his neck, ran her fingers idly through his hair. 'Not even me?' she said huskily, teasingly.

'Not even you, Jezebel.' Lance put his hands round her waist, so slim that he could almost span it. His face changed, grew hungry. His hands tightened and he kissed her.

'Oh! Oh, I beg your pardon!'

Abby opened her eyes in time to see Lance's assistant secretary's startled face as she hurriedly backed out of the room. 'Oh, lor! I didn't hear her knock, did you?'

'No. Where were we?' Lance seemed quite unperturbed as he drew her towards him again.

'Lance!' Abby laughingly pushed him away. 'Don't you realise it will be all over this building in next to no time?'

'What will?'

'The fact that you were caught kissing me, of course.'

He shrugged, 'So?'

'So don't you care? Or do you make a habit of kissing all your girl-friends in your office?' Abby remarked tartly.

'I've never brought a girl-friend here before.'

'Never?'

'Not for many years. And I don't care who sees me.' He kissed her again, lingeringly, until she pulled away, heightened colour in her face.

'Well, I care. I bet everyone in the place thinks I'm . . .' she broke off abruptly.

Lance looked amused. 'That we're lovers?'

'Yes.' Abby flushed.

'Would that be so terrible?' Putting up a finger, he began to trace along her lips.

They were getting on to dangerous ground again. She knew that she ought to move away, bring the conversation down to a saner level, but just the touch of his finger awoke desire in her. She pressed her lips against his hand, kissing his fingers, trying to bite them.

'Abby!'

She raised half-closed, sensuous eyes to see him staring down at her, an arrested look in his grey eyes. He started to say something, but then the buzzer on his desk reverberated through the room. Lance swore, but had to let her go.

He had a small cloakroom opening off his office and Abby went and shut herself in there, looking at her reflection in the mirror and cursing herself for a fool. How on earth could she be so stupid? She'd had him at arm's length and by her own folly had let everything get charged with emotion again. All because she couldn't control her own body, her own desire. Slowly she tidied her hair, put on more lipstick and added more colour to her cheeks to try to disguise the paleness of her skin.

She did her best, but when she came out she was relieved to see that Lance was still on the phone. He smiled and beckoned her over, putting his arm around her waist while he went on talking. Abby supposed she ought to try and listen, but she didn't, was content just to lean against him until he'd finished.

'Sorry about all this, darling; it's one of those crises that crop up in business now and again.'

'It's all right, I understand. But, Lance, would you mind if we called off our plans for today? I have this silly headache and I . . .'

He was immediately all concern, offering to send for the nurse and trying to make her lie down on the settee.

'No, really. It's not that serious. I'm sure it

will go off soon if I just go home and rest for a while.'

Lance yielded in the end, but insisted on taking her down and seeing her into his car himself. 'You look very pale. Are you sure you're going to be all right by yourself?'

'Yes, I'm sure I'll be fine by tomorrow.' She smiled. 'I must be; it's the day they're auctioning the Sarah Bernhardt necklace!'

Lance kissed her lightly right in front of his chauffeur. 'Promise me you'll phone if you feel at all ill?'

He let her go at last and Abby sank back into the seat and closed her eyes, the headache not at all faked, infinitely grateful for the smoothness of the car and the swiftness with which it carried her through the busy streets. As soon as she got into the flat, she swallowed some aspirins, stripped off her outer clothes and lay down on the bed, the curtains closed against the May sunlight. She tried to sleep, but her mind was too restless, going over the past few weeks, wondering about the future. It couldn't be long now before Lance was unmasked. She tried to imagine how he would take it, what he would do. Perhaps he would try and skip the country, let his co-directors take the blame and try to pick up the pieces of the mess he'd left behind him. Would he guess her part in it? she wondered. Would he try and come after her, hot for revenge, as he had with Sarah Bradbury? But she would be long gone by the time he found out, lost in her own world of show business again.

In her imagination, Abby saw it all. Her head ached intolerably; it felt as if someone was tightening an iron band around her head. Sudden hot tears ran down her face and she brushed them angrily away. God, what was happening to her? She felt as if she wasn't in control of her own body any more. She had little time for weakness in others and none at all for it in herself. And yet here was her silly body betraying her at every turn. Recklessly she picked up the bottle of aspirins and swallowed two more, longing for sleep. She hadn't had a sound sleep for quite some time, so when at length it came she slept heavily, so heavily that she didn't hear the phone ringing a few hours later. It stopped, then rang again ten minutes later, and a third time ten minutes after that.

Abby didn't know when she became aware that there was someone in the room with her. Perhaps some primitive instinct warned her, because the moment she woke she knew that there was someone there, and the next that it was Lance. She opened her eyes but didn't move. The room was in semi-darkness, the red light of late evening filtering through the curtains. She could see the outline of his tall figure a few feet away. He was standing still, watching her, that bleak, brooding look on his face. When he saw her open her eyes, he came over to stand beside the bed, but he didn't speak at first. A current seemed to be flowing between them, stronger than anything she had ever known, primeval in its intensity. It was the most forceful non-sexual emotion she had ever experienced. She was afraid to speak or to move, could only lie there, waiting.

He must have seen her fear but mistook the reason for it. 'It's all right, Abby. Don't be afraid—it's Lance.'

Slowly, her taut nerves relaxed. 'I—I don't understand. What are you doing here? How did you get in?'

He sat down beside her on the bed. 'I made your caretaker let me in. You didn't answer your phone and I was worried about you.'

'Didn't I? I didn't hear it. I must have been asleep—I took some aspirins.' She tried to sit up and realised that she was wearing only a black bra-slip with a pair of bikini pants underneath, and the slip had ridden up around her waist. Hurriedly she pulled it down.

Lance gently pushed her down on to the pillows again. 'You've been crying?' His voice was puzzled, questioning.

'It's only this stupid headache. I must look a mess.' Putting a hand up to her eyes, she tried to wipe away all traces of her tears.

His eyes ran down her slim body. 'You look very lovely. Why don't you get undressed and go to bed properly instead of lying on it?'

Abby wondered if that was a proposition and decided she would worry about it later. 'All right.' Going into the bathroom, she cleansed the make-up off her face, then showered and put on a white silk nightdress with a matching négligé, which was the only good one she had. It hadn't seemed right to spend Charles Bradbury's money on expensive night things that Lance would never see—or at least that she had thought he would never see. When she went back into the bedroom he was waiting for her—with a cup of hot chocolate. Which was so out of character that she laughed aloud.

Lance's left eyebrow rose. 'What's so funny?'

'I'm sorry, it's just that I never pictured you playing nursemaid to anyone.'

'No? What did you expect?' He read the answer in her face and his mouth twisted wryly. 'I seem to have given you some wrong ideas about me. You're really quite safe. Didn't I tell you before that I didn't want to spoil things? For heaven's sake come and get into bed, woman,' he added tersely when she still hesitated.

Abby smiled and moved to obey him, her bare toes sinking into the thick softness of the carpet. Lance turned down the bed for her and then tucked her in. 'Here, drink your chocolate. How many pills did you take?'

'About five or six; not all at once. And they were only aspirins.' She indicated the bottle on the bedside cabinet.

'Better not take any more, though. How's your head now?'

'It's getting better. Really. I'm sorry I spoilt our evening.'

'My dear girl! As if that matters. I . . .' He put a hand out to cover hers as it lay on the duvet, but Abby jumped and jerked her hand away so quickly that she spilled the chocolate. Lance stared at her, a grim look about his eyes, 'Do you find my touch so repulsive?'

'No, of course I don't. You know it isn't that.' She gave him a fleeting glance under her lashes and then looked away.

'Do I? Then what is it, Abby?' She wouldn't answer him, so he took the chocolate from her and then put a hand under her chin and forced her to look at him. The grimness was gone, replaced by amused mockery—whether at her or at himself she didn't know. 'You know, Abby, there seems to be only one solution to the situation we find ourselves in.'

'Th-there does?'

'Yes.' He leant forward and kissed her very

lightly on the tip of her nose, then on her lips, hardly touching them. 'I think we'd better get married—and just as soon as possible. Don't you?'

CHAPTER SIX

ABBY's jaw dropped and she stared at him incredulously, sure that she hadn't heard him properly. 'What—what did you say?'

His amusement deepened. 'I asked you to marry me,' he repeated matter-of-factly.

'But you—you can't mean it!' Abby exclaimed.

'I assure you I do. I was never more serious about anything in my life. But I didn't quite expect this reaction,' he admitted ruefully. 'Surely you expected this, darling?'

Abby desperately tried to pull herself together. 'No. I–I told you I wasn't interested in marriage.'

'Nor was I—until I met you.'

Her head began to throb again and she put her fingers up to her temples. 'It's so unexpected. I—I don't know what to say.'

'Then don't say anything, not now. I'm sorry, I've made your headache worse. I didn't intend to say anything tonight, but you seemed so uptight. I thought that perhaps I'd better reassure you about my intentions.' Lance spoke lightly and waited for her to answer, but when she didn't, he got to his feet. 'I don't want to leave, but if I don't your caretaker will gossip. Try to sleep again, darling.' Bending forward, he kissed her on the forehead, but still she didn't say anything or look at him. 'I'll call you tomorrow morning to see if you feel up to going to the sale.'

Try to sleep, he'd said. As if that would be possible now! Abby laughed mirthlessly as she lay

back on the pillows. *Now* what was she going to
do? She had guessed he was falling in love with
her, but had never reasoned it out this far. Why,
she'd only known him for two months—less than
that, even. The man had no right to ask her to
marry him when she'd known him such a short
time. Inevitably she imagined what it would be like
to be married to Lance, to live with him in that
lovely mansion in Kent, to be given everything she
wanted and more. To go to bed with him, have his
hands and lips on her body, feel him making love
to her.

Abby turned her face into the pillow, her body
on fire. It was so easy to fall into the trap. But
there were two sides to Lance and she was
dreaming only about the side that he showed her.
Never, never must she forget his cruel, sadistic side
that had taken revenge on an innocent girl and left
her a mindless vegetable. She guessed, too, that he
would be extremely jealous and possessive, and
shivered at the thought of what he might do if any
girl who had promised herself to him even looked
at another man.

It was many hours before Abby fell asleep
again, and even then it wasn't a restful sleep, so
that she woke feeling dull and heavy headed. It
was late, almost nine-thirty, and her first thought
was that she must get in touch with Charles
Bradbury, but before she could phone him he
called her, barely controlled excitement in his
voice.

'We may have found something,' he told her
before she could speak. 'Do you remember you
read out the titles of the files on Lazenby's desk?
Well, one was headed "Projected Take-over". And
in his tray there was a letter from a firm called

Tewson & Newbury. We think the two may be connected. You must place the bugs in his office right away.'

'I already have,' Abby told him tiredly. 'I did it yesterday.'

'Why didn't you let me know at once?'

'I couldn't.' She thought of explaining, then changed her mind. 'Look, I have to see you.'

'Is it urgent?'

'Yes, very.'

'Can't you tell me over the phone?'

'I'd rather see you.'

'All right.' He didn't sound too pleased. 'You're going to that sale with him today, aren't you? Oh, you can bid up to fifteen thousand, by the way. You'd better phone me again as soon as you're alone and we'll arrange to meet somewhere.'

'Thank you. You're right about the take-over, he told me only yesterday.'

'Did he tell you which company is involved?'

'No. I asked him, but he wouldn't say.'

'You *must* find out, and as soon as possible. It's vitally important. Do you understand?'

Abby assured him that she did and rang off, but had hardly turned away before it rang again. This time it was Lance.

'Good morning, darling. How's the head today?'

'Oh, I'm fine now, thank you,' she lied.

'Well enough to come to the sale?'

'Yes, of course.'

'Good. I'll pick you up in an hour, if that's okay. I tried to get you before, but the line was engaged,' he remarked, with a definite question in his voice.

'Oh, Lance, I'm sorry. I took the phone off the hook last night and I'm afraid I've only just got up.'

They were a little late arriving at the auction house and the sale room was already crowded. One of the officials found a seat for Abby at the back, but Lance had to stand up behind her. Several lots had already gone through and Abby looked rather anxiously at the catalogue, but luckily they were still in plenty of time for the necklace. Because of its history, it had aroused a good deal of interest and the bidding started off very rapidly. Abby didn't bother to raise her hand until the price reached ten thousand pounds, but there were still several people willing to go higher and it soon reached her limit. Someone bid fifteen thousand five hundred and the auctioneer looked at her enquiringly. 'Against you, madam?' Regretfully Abby shook her head. The bidding went on without her and was finally knocked down for twenty-seven thousand to a name she had never heard before, but as the price was so much higher than the limit Charles Bradbury had given her, she didn't feel too bad about it.

After the sale, they went to the Savoy Grill for lunch, but Abby was doubly on edge all the time, afraid that Lance might refer to his proposal of last night, and eager to get away so that she could phone Mr Bradbury. Lance, however, seemed perfectly at ease and in no hurry to get back to work. He didn't mention marriage again directly, but he talked of future plans for Wimbledon and Ascot, taking it for granted that they would be together, even once or twice speaking of things in the distant future and including her in it. He spoke of Venice, and when she told him she hadn't been there, he said, 'The best way to see it is from the sea. When we go there we'll go by boat at sunset so that your first view of it will be a perfect one.'

Abby was in no fit state to fight him today, so she just let it ride without trying to protest. She picked at her food, which was a sin at the prices they charged in the Savoy, but she had no appetite either. Lance made no comment on her apathy, probably putting it down to her headache yesterday, but every time Abby looked up she found his eyes on her. The meal finished at last and she made the excuse that she wanted to do some shopping in Bond Street, so Lance kissed her goodbye, promising to pick her up at seven that evening to go to the ballet.

As soon as his car was out of sight, Abby rushed back into the Savoy to the public telephones. Mercifully Charles Bradbury was free to meet her almost at once and told her to wait for him in a small sandwich bar down the Edgware Road.

He was late; Abby had drunk two coffees and was a bag of nerves before he turned up. He slid into the booth opposite her, completely out of place in his well-cut City suit. On the surface he seemed the same as ever, but Abby sensed an inner excitement which he couldn't quite conceal.

'I'm very pleased with our progress,' he told her. 'It's almost exactly as I predicted. Lazenby is probably using the firm I told you about, Tewson & Newbury, to work a shares fraud and make himself a small fortune on the stock market.'

'How? By taking them over?'

'Good heavens, no, it's much more complicated than that. He's only using the pretext of a merger as a cover-up. I'm afraid you wouldn't understand even if I explained it to you, my dear. It's really very clever. Even the experts couldn't suspect what he's trying to do. Unless of course they already have their suspicions about him, as I do, and manage to get some inside information.' He leant forward. 'Now, tell me exactly what he said to you about a merger.' Abby repeated what little Lance had said and Mr Bradbury shook his head. 'If only we could get hold of that file!'

'Mr Bradbury?' Abby interrupted his thoughts, her hands twisted nervously together under the table. When he looked at her enquiringly, she said, 'Look, I'm sorry, but I've done everything you asked and now I want out. I just can't go on any more.'

His eyebrows rose. 'But we haven't yet got the final proof that we want,' he protested.

'But you're on the right track, and now that all the . . .' she lowered her voice, 'all the bugs are in place you'll soon learn all you need to know.'

'I take it that something has happened to make you want to give up. Has Lazenby made—er—indecent advances to you?'

Abby was too uptight to even think his choice of words funny. 'No, it's not that. It—it's worse. He's asked me to marry him.'

'Good heavens!' Charles Bradbury was so astonished that his glasses fell down his nose. He pushed them back, exclaiming, 'But this is a most tremendous piece of luck! He's played right into our hands.'

Abby's eyes widened as she stared at him. 'What do you mean—a piece of luck? You don't think I'm going to accept him, do you?'

'Why not? The whole object of this exercise was to get close to him. And who could be closer to him than his fiancée?'

'But—but that's crazy!' she retorted angrily. 'I couldn't learn any more than I have already. And just think what kind of position it would put me in.'

'I am,' Bradbury answered immediately. 'It would put you in a position where you could get hold of that file about the take-over.'

'No, it wouldn't; he keeps that in the safe.'

'Not all the time. You saw it once, you can get hold of it again. And if he keeps it in the safe . . .' he shrugged, 'then you must persuade him to programme you so that you can open it.'

She stared at him in mounting horror. 'You're asking me to burgle his safe! You promised that I wouldn't have to do anything like that—nothing illegal, you said.'

Bradbury looked at her over his glasses. 'I'm afraid, Miss Stevens, that you're already committed. Unfortunately I made a mistake; it seems that planting the bugs was against the law, after all.'

'And you let me go ahead and do it? How could you?' she demanded furiously. 'Do you really think that your daughter would want you to stoop so low for her sake?'

He was silent for a long moment, blinking at her behind his glasses, then, 'Unfortunately my daughter can never now have any say in the matter,' he answered shortly. 'She died ten days ago.'

'Oh! Oh, I'm so sorry.' His matter-of-fact statement completely took the wind out of her sails.

'You're right, of course, Miss Stevens,' Bradbury went on before she could recover. 'I'm afraid I've become rather obsessive about this, but now I think you'll understand why. And all we need to end this is a look at that file. It should be really

quite easy, quite simple. I wouldn't want you to
try it if it was at all dangerous.' His voice went on,
soothingly, making it all sound so easy, promising
it would soon be over. 'And I will, of course,
substantially increase your fee,' he murmured.

Abby glared at him. 'I just want to get out. To
be done with all this.'

'Impossible. I'm afraid that at the moment you
have no choice. You must become engaged to him.
I'm sure that as you've managed to hold him at
arm's length this long you will be able to continue
to do so for as long as it takes to get hold of that
file.' He let that sink in, then said, 'Here's a cheque
to cover your expenses to date. Well, I think that's
all. Good day, Miss Stevens.' He gave her a polite
nod, picked up his hat, and walked away.

Abby watched him go, then sat for a long time
just staring down at the table. Slowly she picked up
the cheque he had left for her, looked at it, then
tore it through again and again until the pieces
were so small that they looked like confetti
scattered across the tabletop.

That evening she wore black because it matched
her mood; a beautiful off-the-shoulder dress that
somehow gathered round her hips so that it
accentuated her figure and yet also looked
feminine and elegant. Lance called for her on time,
tall and very handsome in evening dress. Any
woman would have been proud to be seen out with
him, Abby thought as she opened the door, would
be even more proud to call him their fiancé, their
husband. She felt as if she was trapped, like a
rabbit running frantically to get away from a fox,
only to find that whichever way it ran the way was
blocked. She was caught between the ambitions of
two men; one to possess her, the other to use her.

She wanted to cry out against being here but all she could do was to smile a welcome and let Lance kiss her, and tell her how lovely she looked.

'Black suits you, but then you look beautiful in any colour. Although I've noticed you never wear green.'

She shrugged. 'Green is unlucky.'

'I didn't put you down as being superstitious.'

'Perhaps you don't know me very well,' Abby said lightly.

'Don't I?' Lance came and put his hands on her bare shoulders, his eyes looking into hers intently. 'What don't I know about you, Abby?'

She gazed up at him, feeling the strength and warmth of his hands on her skin. Suddenly she wanted to tell him everything. To warn him to give up the fraud before it was too late. To save himself if he could. But then the picture of poor dead Sarah Bradbury filled her mind and she trembled violently.

Lance smiled. 'Somebody walk over your grave again?'

She shook her head. 'No, not mine. Someone else's.'

His left eyebrow rose in surprise, but she had herself well in hand now and laughed up at him. 'How serious we are! What will you have to drink? Gin and tonic, as usual?'

'In a moment. First—I wanted to give you this.' He took a jeweller's case from his pocket and put it in her hands. Abby looked at him questioningly and he said, 'An engagement present.'

'But, Lance, I haven't said I . . .'

'Open it,' he commanded.

Slowly Abby obeyed—and nearly dropped the box when she saw the Sarah Bernhardt necklace lying against the white silk, its jewels flashing red and green and brilliant blue against the gold. 'Oh, my God! Lance, you can't give this to me!' She tried to push the box back at him, but he only laughed and wouldn't take it. 'Lance, please! I can't ... you can't ... I have no right to wear this!'

'Why not?'

'Because ...' Again she was on the point of telling him the truth, but again the fear of his reaction held her back. 'Because we're not engaged,' she finished.

Lance gave a small sigh which she took to be disappointment. 'Wear it for me anyway,' he said lightly. 'It will look beautiful with that dress.'

'I don't understand; how did you get it?'

'When you dropped out I asked one of the officials to go on bidding for me and so his name was called out at the end. I wanted it to be a surprise, you see. Here, let me put it on for you. Turn round.'

She did so, and he unhooked the choker of hired pearls that she was wearing. Then he fastened the serpent necklace in its place, the tail venturing up her throat, its head snaking down towards the valley between her breasts. Lance drew Abby to the mirror and stood behind her, his hands on her waist. The necklace didn't compete against her own beauty, it added to it, accentuating her slim neck and the whiteness of her skin, adding fire to her hair and her eyes.

'Dear God, you're lovely!' Lance's eyes met hers in the mirror. His hands tightened on her waist. 'I want you,' he said suddenly, his voice harsh. 'I want you more than any woman I've ever known.'

Her eyes widened and impulsively she said,

'More than . . .' then hesitated and went on more slowly, 'More than your fiancée who was killed?'

'Yes,' he answered on a soft note of surprise, as if he couldn't quite believe it himself. 'Even more than her.' His hands moved up her arms and he bent to kiss her neck. 'Do you know what it means to a man,' he murmured as he worked his way up towards her ear, 'to want a woman as much as I want you?'

Abby closed her eyes and tilted her head back; the softness of his lips against her skin was sensuously delightful. She wanted it to go on and on. 'Yes,' she whispered, 'I think so.'

His hands moved down to cup her breasts and even through the silk of her dress his touch aroused crazy sensations in her so that she arched her back and moved against his hands. 'Say yes soon, Abby,' he whispered between kisses, his breath warm on her skin. 'Say that you'll be my wife.'

Opening her eyes, Abby slowly turned to face him. 'Why do you want to marry me, Lance?' she asked steadily.

His brows drew together in a quick frown. 'Surely that goes without saying.'

'No. No, it doesn't.'

He stared at her for a moment, then, so slowly that it sounded reluctant, said, 'Because I love you, of course.'

She had expected his face to soften as he said it, but it didn't; instead growing harder, his jaw thrust forward into a stony line. His voice, too, was grim and unyielding.

Abby gazed up at him in surprise. Did it, then, cost him so much effort to admit that he was in love? He had been willing enough to admit that he wanted her, but she was sure he would never have owned to the stronger emotion if she hadn't forced him to do so. Which was strange; she hadn't thought him the kind of man to be afraid of his own emotions.

'All right, Lance,' Abby said in a small, detached voice, 'I will marry you.'

His reaction then was everything that she'd expected it to be. He kissed her passionately, then picked her up by the waist and swung her round. 'Now we really have something to celebrate! Let's forget the ballet and go dancing instead—I want to hold you close to me.'

Abby smiled. 'We could go on to a night-club after the ballet. There's plenty of time. We could dance, then, couldn't we?'

He needed little persuading, and of course she had her way; she had a feeling that he would have given her the earth that night if she'd asked for it. So they went to the ballet and they held hands when the lights went down, went to the bar in the interval and sat with their heads close together, his arm possessively round her waist, as he talked of his plans for the future. At the restaurant they went to afterwards he ordered champagne and raised his glass in a toast, 'To us, my lovely darling.' Again he talked of the future; of the mansion in Kent—if she liked it he would go ahead and buy it, his friends were anxious to leave and it could be ready for them within weeks. And he spoke of their honeymoon, holding her hand across the table and asking her where she would like to go. Anywhere. Anywhere in the world that she wanted to go to. She had only to name the place—and the day.

Abby tried to keep it light; laughing at him and

telling him that it was too soon, they'd only just got engaged, playing for time. They danced, and Lance held her close in his arms as he'd wanted to. She offered no resistance, her arm around his neck, the other held in his against his chest. For a while, as the music flowed over them, Abby pretended that it was for real, that they were in love and had just declared it to one another, that in a while, when they couldn't bear to be apart any longer, they would leave the music and the lights and go back to her flat where they would slowly undress one another and then make love far into the next day. And as she dreamed, Abby suddenly knew that the dream was what she wanted more than anything else in the world. But the dream would never be reality, this was the closest she would ever come to it. The music came to an end and Lance reluctantly let her go, then exclaimed in surprise when he saw that her eyes were wet with tears. 'My dearest, what is it?'

She shook her head and put up a finger to her eyes, trying to smile. 'It's nothing. I suppose it's because I'm—I'm happy.'

'Darling!' Lance put his arm round her and she hid her face in his shoulder.

He gave her more champagne and made her laugh, but now when he looked at her there was something in his eyes that she couldn't fathom. There seemed to be a pensiveness behind his outward manner, as if his mind was preoccupied. Perhaps, Abby thought rather hysterically, he's already beginning to regret being tied down. But on the surface he was everything a girl could want on a night like this: possessively proud, his eyes on no one but her, full of plans and tender compliments, his hand covering hers at every opportunity, letting the world know that she was his. Until Abby thought that she must have been mistaken; that because she was playing a part she was hypersensitive to Lance's reactions, looking in fact for something that wasn't there. He was just a man who was very much in love and had persuaded the girl into saying yes. And his damnation would be that much the greater when he finally found out the truth.

They left the night-club in the early hours and Lance drove slowly back to her flat, having dispensed with his chauffeur tonight. The night porter was napping in a chair, his feet up on the desk. He half opened his eyes, saw who it was and went back to sleep again, used to seeing them together by now. They looked at each other and smiled in shared amusement. It was hot in the flat; Abby didn't turn the lights on right away, but slipped off her mink jacket and moved over to the French windows giving on to a little balcony and pushed them open. It had rained earlier in the evening, but now the air was warm and there was the scent of washed-clean grass rising from the square below. Even this late there were lights showing in the darkened buildings, lights that sparkled like jewels in the quiet streets. London was said to be a magic city; Abby had never noticed it before, but the magic was there tonight.

Lance came up behind her and they stood together for a little while, then he took her hand and drew her back into the moonlit room, looking tall and satanic in his black suit. As always, his hands went to her hair, unclipping it and letting it fall about her shoulders. He began to kiss her, his mouth hungry for hers, and Abby forgot who and where she was, responded only as a woman to a man—to a man she loves. The dream taking over from reality. She kissed him passionately, moving her body against his, wanting to be closer, closer still. She sighed softly as he wound his hands in her hair, kissed her eyes, her throat, and then moaned as he undid the top of her dress and his lips found her breasts. Abby lay back within his arms, her body aching deep down with desire, the will to resist completely gone.

He straightened up and put his hands on either side of her face, kissing her so fiercely that he hurt her. The room whirled around her head and she clung to him, unashamedly pressing herself against him, deliberately arousing him. Lance groaned, the sound torn from his throat, and he moved to pick her up and carry her into the bedroom. But his sleeve caught on the serpent necklace, the cloth snared on the snake's head. He muttered something and tried to drag the sleeve free, it only became more entangled, so that he had to reach up with his other hand to sort it out. It only took him a minute, but it was long enough for Abby to regain some small degree of sanity. As he went to pick her up again, she stepped backwards and put up her hands to hold him off. Shakily, she said, 'Hey, didn't you say you didn't want to spoil things?'

Lance had been reaching out for her, but now he paused. 'We're engaged,' he said thickly. 'How can we spoil anything now?'

She laughed nervously. 'I suppose you'll think I'm silly and old-fashioned, but—well, now I want to wait, Lance. Until we're married. It won't be long, just a few weeks. And—and I'll be so much more relaxed then. I won't feel guilty or—or cheap or anything.' She lowered her head, wildly hoping that a promise of a better time in the future would work, then realised that her breasts were showing and hastily put her arms across them.

Lance immediately stepped forward, took hold of her wrists and forced her arms down. 'Don't ever cover yourself in front of me again,' he said harshly. He looked at her for a moment and then deliberately bent to kiss each of her breasts in turn, taking his time about it, the insistence of his mouth playing havoc with all her good intentions.

Abby stood rigidly, trying desperately not to let it get to her, not to moan or sigh or tell him that she didn't mean it, that she wanted him to go on— and on.

At last he raised his head, his eyes dark. 'There's nothing cheap between us, Abby.' For a moment she thought he was going to force the issue, but instead he let go of her wrists and gently pulled up her dress, covering her. 'I want you, darling,' he told her softly. 'But if you want to wait ...' He shrugged. 'This must be on your terms.'

'Thank you.' She put out a hand and gently touched his. 'I want you, too.' Which, God help her, was the only true thing she'd ever said to him.

He turned to go and Abby walked with him to the door. 'I'll call you tomorrow. We'll meet for lunch.'

'All right.' She reached up and put her arms round his neck. Now that she knew it was safe she could afford to be generous. 'Lance, you're not angry with me, are you? What we have is special; I know that, too. And our wedding—I want it to be perfect, for both of us.'

'Of course, darling, I understand. And I promise you I'm not angry.' He laughed, self-mockingly. 'Just damnably frustrated. I'm going to need a hell of a lot of cold showers between now and our wedding!'

'Idiot!' Abby laughed with him, then she put her hands on his shoulders and reached up to kiss him gently on the mouth. 'Goodnight, Lance.'

'Goodnight.'

She had expected a passionate response, but he merely stood and let her kiss him, not even putting his arms round her. Abby smiled uncertainly, then he opened the door and went quietly away.

She closed the door behind him and leant against it, breathing a long-drawn-out-sigh of relief. It had been so close, so close. She suddenly shivered convulsively, feeling terribly cold despite the warmth of the night. With a sob she ran into the bathroom, tore off her clothes and stepped under the shower, running the water as hot as she could bear it. She lifted her head to the jetting water, wanting to drown beneath it, feeling more wretched and miserable than she had ever done in her life. How long she stood under the shower she didn't know; it must have been a long time, but eventually Abby turned it off and, wrapping herself in a huge bath-sheet, went and lay on the bed. Strangely she didn't feel tired, just terribly lethargic; she wished she could just lie here like a cocoon and hibernate, or whatever it was that cocoons did, not waking up for a long, long time and then being an entirely different person.

As she lay there, her thoughts always on Lance, Abby began to wonder why he hadn't told her that he loved her until she had more or less forced him to say it. Surely that was the first thing a man told a girl when he asked her to marry him—or just to go to bed with him. It had happened to Abby several times in the past, and always the man had told her he was in love with her—most of the times it had even been true. But Lance hadn't. Why? He certainly wasn't shy or unsure of himself; no one could be more the opposite. And he must have been pretty sure of her by then. So why? Abby puzzled over it until the dawn became day, but it was only as she was dropping asleep from sheer exhaustion that it occurred to her that he had never once asked her if *she* loved him!

The insistent bleep of the phone roused her several hours later. More asleep than awake, she reached out and put the receiver to her ear, still nestled under the duvet. 'Hallo,' she muttered.

Lance's voice greeted her. 'You sound as if you're still asleep.'

'I am.'

He laughed. 'Do you know what the time is?'

'No, but I bet you're going to tell me.'

'It's eleven-thirty.' Even over the phone she could hear the amusement in his voice. 'Are you going to get up, or do I have to come over there and drag you out of bed?'

'Oh, God, Lance, how can you be so *bright* after last night?'

His tone changed, grew soft. 'Possibly because last night was the most wonderful in my life—and will be until our wedding day,' he added.

But he meant wedding night, Abby thought. The wedding *day* is for the woman, the *night* for the man.

'Will you come and meet me at the office?' he was saying. 'I'll send the car for you in an hour.'

Abby sat up in bed and realised she was naked. She groaned and padded out to the bathroom, looking critically at herself in the full-length mirror. Her skin was very pale, it was about time she went to a solarium and got herself a tan; she could only just make out the white bikini mark on her behind from last year. Putting her hands on her waist, she ran them down her hips, looking at her long, slim figure dispassionately. The good food and lazy life had made her start to put on weight like a sleek cat, but she was losing it again now. The strain was beginning to show, too, in her face. She had always been fine-boned, but now there were hollows under her cheeks and the bags under her sleep-starved eyes were as big as suitcases. Added to which, she'd gone to sleep with her hair wet and it had gone into waves, like a long, soft afro style.

She did her best, putting on a matching skirt and top in a pretty, light Laura Ashley print, the skirt very full, the top with three-quarter batwing sleeves, casually unbuttoned at the neck. Some of her hair she pulled to one side, did a short plait and tied it with a ribbon. Then she added dark glasses to hide the bags and put all her things into a pretty basket-type handbag. There. Abby looked in the mirror again. A London shepherdess straight out of the latest edition of *Vogue*.

The car had been waiting for her over a quarter of an hour before she was ready. She apologised to the chauffeur for keeping him waiting, and he looked surprised and pleased that she'd bothered. When they got to the City she asked him to telephone ahead, and when they reached Lance's building she didn't go in but waited for him in the car. She supposed she should have gone up to his office and tried to sneak a look at the file on the take-over project, but she couldn't, not today. She didn't want to let Charles Bradbury down and she wanted to do her best to earn the money he was paying her, but she couldn't do it—not today. Not only that, but Bradbury's manner towards her the

last time they'd met had been strange—one
moment pleading, the next threatening, but
perhaps that could be explained by his daughter's
death; it was bound to have unhinged him a
little. But when she had wanted to back out he
had also said that he had made a mistake, that
planting the bugs was illegal after all, and that
there was no way she could back down now.
That had definitely been threatening, almost like
blackmail. Abby wished she knew the truth but
could think of no way to find out. You couldn't
just go up to a policeman or a solicitor or
someone like that and ask them—they might
conceivably want to know why you were so
interested in industrial espionage!

Lance's arrival put a temporary end to her
worrying. He got in beside her and, after kissing
her, asked, 'Why didn't you come up to the office?'

'All your staff look at me so curiously. They
scare me to death!'

He laughed. 'They're only interested. They just
want to see the beautiful girl who's brought their
boss to his knees at last.'

Abby pretended to frown. 'I didn't notice you
getting down on your knees.'

'I was there in spirit, believe me.' Taking her
hand, he said, 'Why have you got those dark
glasses on? Take them off so that I can kiss you
properly.'

'In that case I shall keep them on,' Abby
retorted, lessening it with a smile. 'You've got to
learn to restrain yourself in public.'

His left eyebrow rose. 'Only in public?'

She caught her breath at the way he looked at
her. 'And in private, too. Just for a little while.'

Lance smiled and lifted her hand to his mouth

to kiss her fingers coupled in his. 'I was only teasing. A promise is a promise.'

After lunch he took her to a jeweller's in Hatton Garden and there the most breathtaking of stones were brought out to show her: diamonds of every cut, pulsating with life against the black velvet, rubies and emeralds, blue and yellow sapphires. Lance told her to choose whatever she wanted to be made up into a ring, the jeweller showing her dozens of different designs to take the stones. The guilt at being there under false pretences added to her bewilderment; Abby could only look at Lance helplessly, so he picked out a few designs he thought would suit her. In the end she settled for a square-cut sapphire in an unusual setting with a cluster of small diamonds set on either side.

The jeweller promised to have it ready within a few days, and when they came out Lance said to her, 'I thought of getting you an antique ring, but decided I wanted you to have one that was completely new, that would mean something to you alone.'

'Oh, Lance!' She turned to him, hasty words on her lips, feeling that she couldn't go through with this any more, that she had to tell him the truth. But he was watching her with such an intent, searching look on his face that it brought her up short. She tried to imagine what would happen if she told him here, in the street, after they'd just been choosing an engagement ring, and her heart failed her.

'Yes?' he asked quickly. 'What is it?'

'Nothing.' She shrugged. 'Just—Lance, that's all.'

He smiled rather thinly, but tucked her arm into his. 'Let's walk for a while, shall we?'

It was a beautiful day, the sun shining down out of a cloudless sky, the sort of day when love was in the air, and all the young couples were arm in arm, their heads close together. In the park they strolled through there were more couples, seated on the park benches or on the grass, many of them in a close embrace, indifferent to the passers-by. Abby looked at one pair who were obviously quite oblivious to their surroundings, their arms around each other as they hugged and kissed, then quickly turned her head away.

'Do they embarrass you?' Lance asked her.

She raised her eyes to his and again met that watchful look. 'No.' She shook her head, thinking that she had been like that herself once, when she was young and it was springtime. But that had been eons of time ago. Now she felt terribly old, as if youth had passed her by and she had lost it for ever; which was a hell of a way to feel when you were only twenty-three years old.

CHAPTER SEVEN

THE next day Abby came down with a cold and used it as an excuse not to see Lance and to keep Charles Bradbury off her back. She stayed at home, hiring a sun-bed and lying under it until she got a great tan. It seemed to do her cold good, too, because she was over it in a couple of days. Lance phoned her continuously and filled her flat with flowers and baskets of fruit, but she refused to let him come round, telling him that no way was she going to let him see her looking that terrible. He protested, but she had her way and managed to make the cold excuse last for another two days before he absolutely insisted on coming round. Charles Bradbury, too, had sent her some flowers along with a note wishing her soon well—but then he had his own reasons for wanting her to be better quickly.

Lance raised his eyebrows when he saw her tan. 'If I hadn't spoken to you on the phone every day, I'd say you'd been to the south of France instead of here in the flat!'

Abby smiled. 'I cheated. I hired a sun-bed.'

'With fantastic results.' Drawing her into the room, he took her left hand in his. 'Here, I have something for you.' Taking the engagement ring from his pocket, he slid it on to her third finger.

It looked very good against her newly-tanned skin, the gems, set in platinum, scintillating in the sunlight from the window. Abby became aware that Lance was waiting for her to say something and she had to think herself into the character she was playing, find words for the part. 'It's beautiful, perfect,' she said, with just the right amount of emotion. 'Thank you so much, Lance. I shall wear it always.' Then she smiled and stood on tiptoe to kiss him.

'You're looking thinner,' he remarked afterwards, his finger running down the curve of her cheek. 'You must take care of yourself.' Sitting down on the settee, he pulled her down beside him. 'These last few days have seemed endless without you. I've missed you so much. Don't ever leave me, Abby,' he said lightly. 'I couldn't stand it without you.'

'And I've missed you,' Abby said truthfully, but knowing that it was harder to be near him than apart.

'Well, at least now that you're wearing my ring we can make our engagement official. I'll send the announcement to the paper tomorrow.'

'Announcement?' She looked at him in consternation. 'But do you have to? Surely that isn't necessary?'

His eyebrows came up. 'Not necessary, no, but it's usual, darling. And besides, I want everyone to know just how lucky I am.'

'But—but I don't know anyone in London, hardly.' She searched her brain for an excuse. 'And sending notices to the papers is pretty medieval, Lance; only old squares do that kind of thing any more.'

He burst out laughing. 'Good heavens, I should hate to be accused of being an old square! But although you may not know many people in London, I know a great deal. And I want them to know about us.'

'Well, can't you just tell them? Please, Lance, do we have to make a big thing of this?'

'It is a big thing. But I suppose you told all your friends that you'd never get married and you don't want them to know that you've—shall we say, succumbed to an outdated tradition?'

Abby grabbed the excuse he'd given her greedily. She smiled rather ruefully and leant towards him, looking at him under her lashes. 'I know it's silly, but . . . well, you do understand, don't you?'

'Oh, yes,' he said in a strangely cold tone. 'I understand very well.' Then he smiled and kissed her on the nose. 'All right, darling, I'll hold back the official announcement for a couple of weeks to give you time to get used to the idea. But it goes in at least a month before we're married. Okay?'

'Okay.' Abby smiled at him, thinking that she could always get him to delay it again if she had to, and thanking her stars she had been successful. The anouncement of her engagement would have aroused great interest among her wide circle of friends and fellow actors, and if a certain middle-aged couple living in Jersey had happened to see it, it would have given them quite a surprise to learn that their only daughter was going to marry a man they'd never heard of.

If Abby's life as Lance Lazenby's girl-friend had been an exciting one, life as his fiancée was even more so. He took her to a ball at his old college, to the Derby and later to Ascot where he hired a private box, to a private viewing day at the Royal Academy, to Henley for the Regatta, and they sat in comfortable debenture seats at Wimbledon to watch the tennis. It was a wonderful time and Abby should have enjoyed every minute of it, but she could never relax enough to do so. There was always the knowledge at the back of her mind that she was there under false pretences, that behind their rich, good-looking jet-set couple image was a double sham, her own obviously, but also the ruthless cruelty that was hidden behind Lance's charming façade.

She knew that it was her job, her duty even, to unmask him, but she kept putting it off, telling herself that there was always tomorrow, that one more day wouldn't make any difference. She was sure now that she was in love with Lance. The knowledge grew on her gradually as she hurried to get ready to meet him, rushed to open the door at the first sound of his ring, looked for him eagerly when she met him in a public place. Or when she lay alone in bed, sleepless, night after night, imagining the police coming to arrest him, the looks on the faces of his fellow directors when they learnt the truth about him, the life he would have to live in prison or in disgrace.

And Charles Bradbury, too, was a constant worry at the back of her mind. He phoned her every single day, pushing her to find the merger file, growing first angry and then downright nasty at her continuous excuses. The bugs, it seemed, hadn't come up to expectations at all, and it was now up to her. She only had to take a quick look at the file, read enough to find out which was the company involved.

To escape from it, Abby started going for long walks when Lance was working. Often she went down to the river and sat looking at the water for hours, or crossed over the Albert Bridge and strolled round the large area of Battersea Park. But more often she walked along the Embankment, past the Royal Hospital for disabled soldiers, where the Chelsea Pensioners in their gay scarlet uniforms lived, to Ranelagh Gardens or to the newly-opened Physick Garden of the Apothecaries Society, where grew all the herbs for all the old wives' remedies ever known. The four walls of the flat seemed to close in on her when she was alone, she needed to be out in the open, to feel free for a while of the part she was playing, but she couldn't escape the indecision that constantly tore at her mind. For a second time she tried to regain some sense of proportion by going back to her old haunts. She ran into several people she knew in the coffee bars and small restaurants around the theatre area in the West End, and once she met Paul Tait, the producer of the television series that she had auditioned for. The series had started to appear and Abby had watched the first episode. Generously she went over to congratulate him.

'Thanks,' he answered. 'The girl we've got now is good, but I'd rather have had you for the part if you'd been free.'

Abby's eyebrows flew up in surprise. 'But I was free; I told you so at the time.'

Paul frowned. 'But when I phoned your agent to fix the details, he said you'd been given a part you'd auditioned for earlier and had to take it.'

'But he told me you wanted someone with more TV experience!'

They parted with Abby full of anger and determined to go and see Tolly and have it out with him. Either he'd made a really bad mistake or he'd done it deliberately, in which case she wanted to know why. She almost went to see him there and then, but halfway to his office realised that she didn't really care any more; compared to the problem that was facing her now, it just didn't matter.

The summer weather in England can play strange tricks; one day being so hot that you bake, the next so cold that you get out your winter woollies again. It was on one of the colder days that Abby sat on a wooden bench overlooking the turgid grey waters of the Thames, huddled into a camel coat, the collar turned up against the wind. Cars passed along the Embankment behind her continuously, heading either for the City or the London docks. She didn't notice when one car went slowly by and then stopped. Quick footsteps crossed the pavement towards her.

'Abby?'

She started nervously and looked up to see Lance standing beside her. 'Oh! Hi.' Glancing round, she saw the Rolls waiting at the kerb, the chauffeur at the wheel. 'Were you passing? We hadn't arranged to meet, had we? I haven't forgotten?'

'No.' He sat down beside her. 'I waited at your flat for some time, but then the porter told me you'd gone for a walk, so I drove down here in the hope of finding you.'

'Was it for something urgent?'

'No. A meeting was cancelled, so I have a couple of free hours. I thought we could have lunch together.' He studied her drawn face for a moment, turned and motioned his chauffeur to leave, then reached down to help her to her feet. 'Let's walk, shall we?'

Abby had her hands pushed into her pockets for warmth. Lance slipped his right arm through her left and they walked slowly along in close proximity. The wind whipped the waters of the river in white-crested waves. Boats pulled uneasily at their moorings or battled their way down river to the sea. It caught at Abby's hair and loosened soft tendrils on to her cheeks, and blew a dark lock forward on to Lance's forehead, making him look younger somehow, less formidable. Perhaps he realised it, because he immediately put up a hand and pushed it back into place.

They walked in silence for some time, but when they reached the shadowed shelter under a bridge Lance paused to light a cigarette. Abby stood near to him, making a little cave of shelter against the wind so that the match wouldn't blow out. The cigarette lit and glowed and she would have moved on, but Lance held her still. 'Is something worrying you, Abby?' he asked, his grey eyes fixed intently on her face.

She tried her best to sound light and uncaring. 'No, of course not. Why should there be?'

'I don't know. But you seem—troubled.'

'Perhaps it's pre-wedding nerves,' she admitted with a laugh that sounded unnatural even to her own ears, a laugh that was picked up by the wind and sent echoing hollowly against the high arch of the bridge above them.

Lance's eyebrows rose in disbelief. 'Really? When you haven't even set a date yet?'

In that second Abby knew that she had to end it, that she couldn't go on playing for time, hoping against hope for something, she didn't know what, to happen, to make everything come right. It wasn't fair to Bradbury, or herself, or even on Lance.

'Would—would the first of August be okay?'

He stared at her, than gave a broad grin. 'The first of August would be marvellous, absolutely marvellous!' Drawing her a little closer, he bent to kiss her.

Abby felt the warmth of his lips against her cold skin and was filled with an uncontrollable longing. Flinging her arms around his neck, she clung to him, kissing him as if it was the last time, as if she would never see him again. Then, just as abruptly, she let him go, stepping back and huddling herself into her coat again. Lance was gazing at her in startled surprise, but before he could speak Abby said hurriedly, 'It's so cold. The wind's making my eyes water. Let's go back now, shall we?'

The Rolls was already outside her building when they got back and Lance waited in it while Abby ran upstairs to tidy herself and get her bag. When she came back and they were driving along, she handed him a spare key to her flat. 'I'm sorry I wasn't in. Perhaps you'd better take this in case you need it any time.'

'Thank you, darling. And you'd better have one to my place.' Reaching into an inside pocket, he fished out two keys on a ring. 'The Yale key is for the main door of my apartment building, the other is for my door.'

Abby smiled and dropped them into her bag, thinking that those weren't the keys she wanted; she needed to get into his office, not his flat. But since that first time, Lance hadn't asked her to meet him there again, so she would have to create an opportunity herself. The next day was a Thursday, they had a date later in the evening, but Abby deliberately went to Lance's office at about five-thirty. The receptionist recognised her at once. 'Why, Miss Stevens! I wasn't told to expect you. Does Mr Lazenby know you're coming?'

'No, I just called in the hope of catching him before he left. Is he still here?' Abby asked innocently, although she knew darn well that he was, because she'd checked that the Rolls was still in the underground car park he used.

'Yes. I'll phone through and tell him you're here.' The girl spoke on the phone and then said, 'He asks if you'd mind going up to his office?'

She looked round for someone to escort her, but Abby said quickly, 'Oh, please don't bother. I can find my own way.' She went up in the lift, her heart beating fast, her hands damp with nerves.

His male secretary was waiting for her when she reached his floor. 'I'm afraid Mr Lazenby is tied up at the moment. Would you mind waiting in his office?'

'No,' Abby answered sincerely, 'of course not.'

'Would you like some coffee?'

She refused it and he excused himself, saying that he had a few things to see to before he left. The door closed behind him and Abby gave a sigh of relief, thanking her stars that it hadn't been his chatty female secretary that Lance had sent to meet her. Quickly she crossed to his desk and began to go through the small stack of files that lay on it. None was the one she wanted, but she could hardly expect to be so lucky a second time. Perhaps it was in one of the drawers. She pulled them out, hurriedly searching through the contents. Still no luck. There were a couple of filing cabinets against the wall which Abby searched as systematically as she could with one eye on the door and her ears strained for any warning noise. She had almost finished the second cabinet when she heard the sound of Lance's voice in the outer office. Hastily she pushed the drawer shut and ran back to a chair, picking up a magazine and finding that she was holding it upside down just in time to turn it before the door opened.

'Hallo, darling. What a lovely surprise.' Lance dropped his brief case on his desk as he bent down to kiss her.

'I hope you don't mind me coming, but I'm in rather a jam.' Abby gave him a rather helpless smile, hoping to appeal to his masculine chivalry.

He grinned indulgently. 'What have you done: bid by mistake at an auction for something you didn't want?'

Abby smiled in return. 'Not quite as bad as that. I went shopping in Knightsbridge and they had one of those mini fashion parades in the store. I stopped to watch it and unfortunately forgot the time. When I came out all the banks were shut and it was too late to cash a cheque. Then I thought that perhaps you might be able to change it for me. Do you keep any cash here?—I don't know.'

'Well, yes, we do. But perhaps I can help out. How much do you need?' He reached into his pocket for his wallet.

'It's rather a large sum, I'm afraid. Two hundred and fifty pounds.'

Lance's left eyebrow rose. 'I don't carry that much around on me, but I'm sure we can find it for you. You're not being blackmailed, are you?' he asked, only half-jokingly.

'Good heavens, no!' Abby laughed in genuine amazement. 'No, unfortunately I dropped a heavy bottle of bubble bath into the handbasin in my bathroom this morning and it broke the basin. At first the plumbers said they couldn't replace it for two weeks, but then I managed to persuade a man to come tomorrow—but he wants cash.'

'I see. Well, there should be enough in the safe if the cashbox is in there yet. We keep quite a bit on the premises in case of emergencies.' Going over to the filing cabinet, he operated the switch that revealed the safe and soon had it open. He walked inside, but came out a minute later. 'It hasn't been brought up yet. I'll go and fetch it.'

'Oh, lor! Am I putting you to an awful lot of bother?'

'Of course not.' Lance tapped her lightly on the nose. 'I can't have you being dunned by tradesmen. Shan't be more than five minutes.' He went out, leaving the safe open behind him.

He left the safe open! Abby gave him twenty seconds to get clear and then dived inside. Oh, God, the place was full of files. But they were mostly the box type, not the manilla folder that she was looking for. She began to scan the titles, which mostly seemed to be the names of companies, and had wasted nearly a minute before she realised they were in alphabetical order. No, there was nothing under Tewson & Newbury, so she turned and feverishly began to go through several baskets of papers. Still no luck. A hurried look at her watch. Three minutes had gone. Only two left. There were several folders on a shelf near the door; Abby pulled them out, but they seemed to hold nothing but share certificates. She put them back as tidily as she could in five seconds flat and looked round wildly. It had to be here, it just had to be! There was a big metal box on the floor. Abby tugged at the handle hopefully but found it locked, then realised there was a light film of dust on the lid and immediately rejected it. Four and a half minutes. Oh, God, where was it? Her eyes sought in vain for the file, it just wasn't there.

Abby came out and stood by the window, biting her lip. Perhaps one of the other directors had the file in his office, in his own safe, in which case she'd never get to see it. She'd banked everything on the file being in Lance's office at this time of night.

'Here we are,' Lance came back and pulled a wad of notes out of his pocket. 'That should keep your plumber sweet.'

'Oh, *thanks*! You've saved my life.' Abby stuffed the money in her bag and took out her cheque book. 'Who shall I make the cheque payable to—you or your company?'

'That isn't necessary, darling, you know that'

'No, please. I must repay you.' She looked at him saucily. 'I'm not your kept woman yet, you know.'

He pretended to leer at her menacingly. 'Just you wait until the first of August!'

Abby's heart skipped a beat, but she laughed. 'Down, boy! Now, seriously, who do I make this out to?'

'To me, then, if you insist.'

While she wrote out the cheque, Lance locked up the safe and rang down for his car. 'All set?' She nodded and handed him the cheque. He took it without looking at it, and opened his briefcase to slip it in. Abby nearly died. Right there, on the top of his other papers, was the take-over file, its title in large letters shrieking out at her. And the case hadn't even been locked! She could have read it and found out everything she wanted.

Lance repeated his question and she managed to nod and smile, feeling sick inside. She had been so close, so very close.

'Let's go then, shall we?' He held the door for

her and she preceded him to the lift, saying goodnight to various people as they went, the whole time trying to work out how she could manage to be alone with his case again. When they got in the car, Lance took her hand in his, idly turning her engagement ring on her finger. 'Bad news, I'm afraid, darling. I have to go up to Edinburgh again tomorrow.'

'For the whole day?'

'I have some work to do first, but I can do that at home, luckily, then I'll catch the shuttle from Heathrow. I might have to stay the night in Scotland, but I'll get back as soon as I can. Sorry, darling, it means I won't be able to take you to see that film, as we'd planned.'

'It doesn't matter—I understand. We can go some other night.' She smiled and glanced out of the windows. 'Where are we going, Lance?'

'What?' He, too, looked out. 'To my place, by the look of it. Sorry, darling, I didn't give the driver any instructions, so he just headed for home. Do you want to go back to your flat?'

'No,' Abby said hastily, remembering that she was supposed to have a broken sink. 'Your place will be fine. Perhaps we could eat at the Belle Auberge again?' she added, naming a French restaurant tucked into a pleasant back street not too far from his flat.

'Of course.' He looked pleased. 'And afterwards?'

'You choose.' She moved closer to him. 'We'll do whatever you want.'

Most other men might have taken that the wrong way, or at least have made some dubious remark, but Lance didn't; he wasn't that kind of man. His fingers merely tightened on hers and he

began to tell her about his trip to Edinburgh.
When they reached his flat, he poured them a
drink, phoned the restaurant to book a table, then
chatted for about twenty minutes while they
drank. He had put his case down on the floor near
his desk and it took all Abby's willpower not to let
her eyes keep straying to it, wishing that Lance
would go away and leave her alone with it for two
minutes—just two minutes was all it would take.
At last he finished his drink, stood up and moved
towards his bedroom door. Abby's pulses began to
race and she willed him to go through it, but on
the threshold he paused, then turned back. 'I'd
better put some things in the safe before I forget.'

To Abby's chagrin, he took the file and several
other papers from his briefcase and took them into
his bedroom where he had a wall safe which was
hidden behind a hinged mirror. Casually she
followed him and leant against the door jamb,
watching him as he twisted the dials.

'I don't know how you can remember those
random numbers,' she remarked offhandedly. 'I'm
always forgetting mine and have to phone up the
makers to find out.'

'But mine aren't random numbers. They're
really quite simple.' He spoke with his back to her.
'It's my birthday, which is the sixteenth of the
twelfth, add the two together making twenty-eight
and divide by two, giving you fourteen. *Et voilà!*'
He opened the safe and pushed the papers in,
closed it again and spun the dial to lock it.

Afterwards he went into the bathroom to shave
and Abby had the wild idea of unlocking the safe
and taking a look at the file while he did so, but
the next moment dismissed the thought as
madness; he hadn't shut the bathroom door and

the room was lined with mirror glass, he would be bound to see her. And anyway, there was now no need to take the risk; he was going away tomorrow and he had very conveniently given her the keys to his flat, and now, too, the combination of his safe. She had only to wait until tomorrow and there would be no danger; it would be easy.

'Pick me out a tie, would you, darling?'

Lance's voice rose above the soft burr of his electric razor and she obediently opened his wardrobe until she found his tie-rack. He had dozens of suits and twice as many ties. Abby chose one and laid it on the bed beside the suit he'd laid out. She'd never been in his bedroom before and she looked round curiously, cynically noting the size of the bed; it was huge, at least king-size, but then Lance was a king-sized man. It was a very masculine room, luxuriously comfortable with a deep-pile carpet, but there were none of the ornaments or pictures that a woman usually has in her bedroom. Except one. There was a photograph on a small table over by the far side of the bed. Curious, Abby walked round and picked it up. It was a colour photo, of a girl who, superficially, looked very like herself, about the same age and with long chestnut hair only a couple of shades redder than her own. But the girl's eyes were brown, not green, and there was a wilful, rather wild look about her mouth. Abby could well imagine her taking a car she couldn't handle just because she'd been told not to. The photo was inscribed: 'To my darling Lance, with all my love for ever,' and then just the initial 'E'.

Abby stood staring down at the picture in her hands; she didn't hear the razor stop or Lance come out of the bathroom. Only his harsh voice cut through her thoughts.

'What are you looking at?'

Slowly she turned. 'This.'

His jaw tightened as he saw. He had put on a clean white shirt which hung open, revealing the dark mat of hairs on his chest.

'I take it this was the girl you were engaged to?' Abby demanded, her voice rising.

He came to take the photo from her, looking at it briefly. 'Yes.'

Sudden violent rage filled her, rage at her own stupidity in falling in love with him as much as anything else. Lifting her right hand, she slapped him hard across the face, then turned and made for the door.

'What the hell was that for?' Lance grabbed her arm and yanked her round to face him, his eyes angry.

'You know darn well what for. Because you're a liar and a cheat! Let go my arm!' She tried to pull away, but he held her firmly.

'What are you talking about?' He caught hold of her other wrist. 'Abby, tell me.'

'Why tell you what you already know?' she yelled at him furiously. 'You don't love me— you're still in love with her. You're just using me as a substitute because I look like her. You louse! Let me go!' Again she tried to pull free.

'That isn't true—I swear it.'

'You liar! I could be her double.'

'Abby, will you listen to me? She's just a memory, nothing more. I stopped grieving for her years ago.'

'I don't believe you. I never want to see you again . . .'

'Oh, for God's sake! There's only one way to get through to you.' Lance suddenly jerked her to him and kissed her, his mouth closing over her protests, shutting out the past and the future, creating a small, whirling world that was here and now, desire and passion mingled. When at last he raised his head, he said unevenly, '*Now* do you believe me? Okay, maybe you do look a bit like her, but if all I'd wanted was a substitute for her do you think I couldn't have found a dozen who look even more like her than you do, in all these years? Really, it's only your hair. And the first time I met you I didn't even see your hair, you had it hidden under a hat. Remember?'

'Oh God!' Abby was leaning against him, her face pressed against the bare column of his throat, her hands on his chest under his shirt. Her eyes were wet and she was trembling, her emotions still raw and naked.

'Tell me you believe me.' Lance held her away from him so that he could see her face. 'Say it,' he insisted.

'I believe you.' She said it rather tiredly and drew away from him. He had thrown the photograph down on the bed and the girl smiled up at her mockingly. 'Why do you still keep her picture if she doesn't mean anything to you any more?'

Lance shrugged. 'It's always been there, has become part of the furniture, I suppose.' He turned her gently round to face him, put up a finger to wipe away a tear that glistened on her lashes. 'Why don't you have one taken so that I can have that instead? Not that I need a photograph to remind me of you—you're always with me, always in my thoughts,' he said caressingly.

'Oh, Lance, hold me—hold me close.'

He did so, his arms around her, and presently, when she had quietened a little, he kissed her again, but gently this time.

Abby broke away first. She put a hand up to her face and said unsteadily, 'Do you mind if I use your bathroom?' She fetched her bag from the sitting-room and then shut herself away, locking the door firmly behind her. For several minutes she just leant her head against the wall, trying to control her emotions. Going off at him like that had been an abysmally stupid thing to do. What did it matter whether he really loved her or not? She could so easily have ruined everything. Slowly she stood up and splashed cold water on to her face, patted it dry and began to apply fresh make-up. Her unhappy face stared back at her, her own face, not that of an actor playing a part. And the worst part of it was she knew full well that whatever Lance's real feelings they weren't for that face at all, they were only for a girl who, either way, didn't exist.

When she came out he was waiting for her, his eyes searching her face in concern, but she gave him a bright smile, apparently fully recovered, and he slowly relaxed. They went to their favourite restaurant, and it was a good evening because Abby was determined to make it so. She was sparkling and witty, making him laugh, and just flirtatious enough to turn him on without overdoing it so that he got serious. She was the kind of beautiful girl every man wants and seldom finds. It had to be that way, because tonight was the last time she would ever see him, the last time she would hear him speak, or feel the touch of his hand. The last time he would smile that slow smile, or raise her fingers to his lips as his eyes looked deep into hers. And she wanted tonight to be perfect, to remember it as it was on the surface, as if it had been real. Just two people who were very much in love.

After the meal Abby said she was tired and he drove her straight home. Lance kissed her goodnight in her flat and somehow she found the strength not to cling to him, but to part as though she would be seeing him again soon. But, despite all her efforts, it seemed that something of her inner sadness had reached him, because he put a hand up to her face and looked at her rather oddly, 'You're sure you're all right?'

'Yes, of course. Hurry back tomorrow. Promise to phone me as soon as you arrive?'

'All right.' But he hesitated a moment longer before saying, 'Goodnight, darling.'

'Goodbye, Lance.'

Going to the window, she waited until he emerged from the entrance, then watched as he got into his car and drove away, looking up to wave to her before he did so. She didn't wave back, just stood and watched him go, wondering why heartbreak should be such a physical pain.

Then she turned away; there was a great deal to be done by tomorrow, because she knew now exactly what she was going to do.

It was two in the afternoon of the next day before Abby rang Lance's flat to make sure that he was well on his way to Scotland. She let it ring for several minutes before she put the receiver down, just to confirm that he wasn't there, then she took a last check round her flat, making sure that she'd left nothing behind. The porter carried her two cases containing her clothes; her own things that she had brought with her in the beginning, down to the waiting taxi, while Abby stuffed the two parcels, one addressed to Charles Bradbury, the other to Lance, into her large, holdall type bag. Also she wore her own jeans and shirt with a jacket over the top, her hair hanging loose and sunglasses covering her eyes.

She didn't go straight to Lance's flat, but went first to her old place in Clapham, where she left her cases. There was no one in and it would probably come as a surprise when she turned up later, but it didn't really matter if they didn't have room for her; Abby didn't much care where she went. From Clapham, the taxi took her back across the Thames, past the walls of Buckingham Palace to Lance's flat. It was quite busy round the entrance, there was a Harrods van outside and the main door stood wide open as the delivery men manoeuvred a large settee into the building. Abby slipped past them as the porter held a lift for them, and headed for the stairs. She didn't meet anyone, not many people bothered with the stairs, and there was no one about in Lance's corridor. Even so, she hesitated and looked about her again before she turned the key in the lock and slipped inside.

The curtains were open and sunlight filled the flat. Abby dropped her bag on the floor by the front door and stepped down into the big sitting-room. It was very quiet. There was no one to hear her, of course, but she walked quietly over to the bedroom and pushed open the door. This room, too, was bright with sunshine; it seemed wrong somehow, as if what she was about to do ought to be done in gloomy murkiness. The little table was empty, the photo of his dead fiancée taken away.

Had he destroyed it? she wondered, but then pushed the thought aside. It hardly mattered any more.

The mirror concealing the safe was part of a built-in dressing-table unit. Abby pulled it open and reached up to the dial, remembering the numbers quite easily: sixteen, twelve, twenty-eight, fourteen. The door clicked open. Abby took out the file, careful not to disturb or even look at anything else. Opening it, she took out the top letter and found out everything she needed to know. Bradbury had been right, Tewson & Newbury was the company Lance was using for his phoney take-over. And from the dates in the letter it seemed that it was due to take place very soon. Crossing to the phone, Abby dialled Bradbury's number and as soon as he came on the line gave him the bald facts. He didn't ask her how she'd found out, how she'd got hold of the file or where she was, he just asked her in a voice of great excitement to read out the letter, then rang off quickly, muttering about catching the market before it closed.

After putting the file back in the safe, Abby closed it and pushed the mirror to, then stood staring at her reflection for a long moment before she turned away. There was just one thing left to do and then she could leave. She started for the front door to find her bag, but as she crossed the sitting-room, the door to the kitchen opened and Lance came through. 'Hallo, Abby,' he said conversationally. 'Surely you're not leaving already? Why don't you stay—and talk?'

CHAPTER EIGHT

ABBY stood in the centre of the room staring at Lance, frozen with shock, and at first it didn't even register that he didn't seem at all surprised to see her there. He just stood watching her, waiting for her to react.

Seeing him again so suddenly, when she thought that she had said goodbye to him for ever, was a big enough shock in itself, to have him find her in his flat was like having a bomb blow up in her face. Somehow, her voice completely ragged, she managed to say, 'Lord, you frightened the wits out of me!'

'Really?' He took a couple of steps into the room. 'Why?'

'Why?' She gave a shaky laugh. 'Because I thought you were in Edinburgh, of course. What happened?' she asked, trying desperately to appear normal but her heart beating like crazy. 'Did you change your mind?'

'No,' Lance replied, but he didn't enlarge on it. 'What are you doing here?'

'I—I brought a parcel for you. It's in my bag; I'll get it.'

She moved towards the door, but his voice cracked like a whip, stopping her dead. 'Later. Why were you in the bedroom?'

Acting for her life, Abby pretended to look rather shamefaced. 'Oh. Well, if you must know, I wanted to see if that photograph was still there. Are you,' she looked at him under her lashes, 'are you very annoyed with me?'

Lance's lip curled. 'No, I'm not—annoyed.'

'Oh. Good.' Abby began to talk fast as she edged towards the door. 'That plumber didn't turn up after all, so I brought you your two hundred and fifty pounds back. I thought it would be safer if I . . .' Her voice trailed away as she watched his face, saw the undisguised contempt in his eyes, and realised with absolute certainty that he knew.

'Oh, please go on,' Lance said scornfully. 'I'm really enjoying your performance. You know, you're really a very good actress. The payment must be really big to make you play a part as low as this.'

The colour flooded from Abby's face. For a minute she was like an animal too petrified to move, but then she saw the menace in his eyes and plunged for the door. Her fingers almost touched the door handle, but then he was on her and dragged her back.

'You bitch! You cold-hearted, cheating little bitch!'

She began to scream, but Lance put a hand in her hair and jerked her head back so that her cry was broken off, then he got hold of one of her wrists and twisted it behind her back. She struggled wildly, kicking out at his ankles, and then she tried to knee him. Immediately he viciously pulled her arm further up her back so that she cried out in pain.

'Just try that once more, Abby, and I'll really start to hurt you!' He sounded as if he wished she would, as if he'd enjoy doing it. His grey eyes blazed down at her murderously and Abby shrank with fear. 'Now, you've got some talking to do. Who was paying you to spy on me? Who was it?'

'I don't ... I don't know what you mean, Lance, I ...' She screamed again and tears came to her eyes as he jerked her arm for a second time.

'You filthy little liar! Who was it? Tell me!'

Shaking with fear, Abby stared up at him, the tears running down her cheeks. He was holding her close against his chest and she could see the sweat of anger on his skin, feel it running through his body. His eyes glared down at her in hot, passionate rage and she knew that to antagonise him further would be suicidal. 'His name is Charles Bradbury,' she answered with a reluctant sob.

Again he showed no surprise or even gratification. 'And who else? Who's in this with him?' he demanded.

'I don't know.' She saw his mouth curl in disbelief and felt his hand tighten on her wrist. 'It's true, I tell you,' she cried in a panic of fear. 'I only know about Bradbury. I don't know if there was anyone else.'

Mercifully he seemed to accept this, because he didn't pursue it, instead saying bitingly, 'How much did he pay you to lie and cheat? Answer me, you worthless little bitch!' he added when she made a move of protest. 'How much?'

'Five—five thousand pounds.'

'And did that include seducing me? Having to sleep with the man you were cheating?' His jaw hardened. 'Or did your price come higher for that?'

'I didn't ... We never ...'

'No. But you would have done,' he said forcefully. 'I found that out when I decided to see just how far you were willing to go to further your scheming. My God, did you really believe I drew back because I didn't want to spoil our beautiful relationship?' he laughed harshly.

'You—you knew? Even then?' Abby could hardly get the words out.

'Of course I knew. I knew almost from the start. Do you think you were the first girl who looked like my fiancée that Bradbury tried to throw in my way? He'd already tried the same thing twice before, but I hadn't taken the bait. This time I decided to follow it up, to find out who and what was behind it. And it took hardly any time at all; you led me straight to Bradbury. Look,' he pulled her over to his desk and yanked open a drawer, took out an envelope of photographs and emptied them out. They were photos of herself with Charles Bradbury in the pub in the Mile End Road and also of their later meeting in the sandwich bar.

Abby stared at them as it began to sink in that he had been playing a part as much as she had, had known all the time, *all the time.* 'So why didn't you end it then?' she burst out in an agony of revulsion. 'Why did you go on—pretending?'

'Because I was getting more than a little tired of Charles Bradbury. I'd grabbed a big order from under his nose a couple of years ago and he couldn't forget it. He tried blackening my name in the City and when that didn't work, began to try even more underhand methods instead. But this time I decided to let him use his own mad greed to ruin himself.'

'What—what do you mean?' Abby stared at him, her heart going cold with dread.

Lance's mouth twisted into a contemptuous sneer. 'There never was any projected merger with Tewson & Newbury. I just planted those letters so

that you'd send the information back to Bradbury.
I even made it easy for you by deliberately taking
you back to my office, and practically spelt the
thing out to you when I gave you the key to this
flat and told you the combination of the safe. I
knew you'd come back today when you thought I
was safely out of the way. And I knew that the
minute you phoned through the information he
wanted, Bradbury would call his broker and buy
in as many Tewson & Newbury shares as he
possibly could. At the moment the price is quite
high, I've seen to that, but he knows that the
minute the take-over is announced those shares
will rocket and he'll make a killing.' He paused,
then said with vicious emphasis, 'What he doesn't
know is that the moment the Stock Exchange
closes today, Tewson & Newbury will go into
liquidation, their shares will be written off and
Bradbury will lose every penny he put into this.'

Her eyes widening in horror, Abby stammered,
'But you—but you can't do that!'

'Why not? The miserable little swine deserves all
that's coming to him. And I'll make sure that he
gets kicked out of the City, too.'

Then, suddenly, Abby's fear left her and she
became passionately, gloriously angry. With a
swift tug that took him completely by surprise, she
freed her wrist and started lashing out at him.
'How dare you say that? How *dare* you? My God,
haven't you done enough to that poor man?'

Lance stepped neatly out of the way as she tried to
kick him, lifting her legs high to get him where it
would really hurt. 'You vicious little cat!' he
exclaimed angrily. 'You fight as dirty as you are!' He
made a lunge for her, but Abby ran to the side of the
room, picked up a heavy book and threw it at him.

'You swine,' she yelled at him. 'I wish it had worked. I wish you'd been ruined and gone to prison! You deserve every minute of it. I wish we'd made you grovel!'

Disgust came into Lance's face. 'So you really care about him, do you?' He made a grab for her again, and Abby moved smartly in the opposite direction, but he had anticipated it and changed course so swiftly that she hardly had a chance to realise what was happening before he caught hold of her arm. She gave a yell of protest and tried to get away again, but he held her easily, laughing at her struggles. 'What's the matter? Do you really think I'm going to let you get away and warn him before it's too late? You must care for him a lot. Because he's your lover, isn't he? You go to bed with that disgusting old . . .'

Pure, red-hot rage filled her and Abby struck at him with her free hand, putting everything she'd got behind it. And this time the blow connected, catching him on the side of the face, so that for a moment he staggered backwards, but he didn't let go of her arm and he recovered within seconds.

In contrast to her hot anger, his eyes filled with a cold, malevolent fury. 'You did that once too often,' he told her breathlessly, then jerked her off balance and caught her as she fell, picking her up in his arms and carrying her, yelling and struggling into the bedroom.

'You pig! You louse! Do you think I don't know what you did to Bradbury's daughter? She's dead because of what you did to her!' Abby's arms were pinned to her sides, but she tried to butt him in the face with her head, the tears of helpless rage pouring down her cheeks.

'Bradbury doesn't have a daughter.'

'You liar! I saw her at the clinic. She was nothing but a cabbage because of what you did to her. And now she's dead. But you don't even care!'

'He isn't even married.' Lance reached the bed and dropped her on to it, then quickly knelt over her, straddling her body, holding her arms down on either side of her head. 'But you're right—I don't care what lies he told you about me; he's already dug his own grave. I don't even care if he fooled you into helping him. Because now this is just between you and me.'

He was breathing heavily from his exertions and his hair had fallen forward over his forehead. She had torn his shirt in her struggles and it hung open to the waist, and there was a red mark on his face where she'd hit him. But it was his eyes that held her; they were as cold as winter frost and just as deadly, filled with a cold-blooded need for revenge.

'No!' The word came out as a choking plea, but he didn't even hear it.

His hand went to her shirt, began to deliberately undo the buttons. 'During this game we've been playing I told you a whole lot of lies to match yours,' he told her with icy venom. 'But there was one thing I said that was the truth. When I told you I wanted you.'

'Oh God, no!' The words came out as a shocked, agonised whisper as she stared up at him, knowing now that this was what he'd intended all along.

'I could have taken you before, of course,' he said with soft savagery. 'At any time. But I wasn't going to drop to your level and pretend an emotion I didn't feel. But now we both know exactly where we stand. And we both know just what this is.' He let go of her other hand so that he could open her shirt. She wasn't wearing anything underneath. His eyes devoured her as he deliberately took his time before he touched her.

Abby made a convulsive movement to cover herself, but he knocked her arms aside and slapped her face just hard enough to make her eyes sting. Then his hands went back to her breasts. 'No! No, Lance, please!' But even as she said the words she knew it was no use. He was set on his revenge and nothing she could say would stop him. She looked wildly round, searching for a way out—anything.

There was a telephone on the cabinet beside the bed; if only she could reach it—but he'd never give her time enough to use it. Beside the phone there was a heavy glass ashtray. Lance moved back a little as his hands went to the fastening of her jeans. Without stopping to think, Abby threw herself sideways, grabbed the ashtray and swung it backwards at his head, all in one movement. At the last second he saw it coming and tried to duck, but it crashed against the right-hand side of his head, narrowly missing his temple with the sharp corner. For a moment, as Abby stared up at him in terrified horror, it seemed as if he wasn't hurt, but then he muttered something she couldn't hear, his eyes glazed over and he pitched forward on top of her, blood beginning to flow from a cut on his head.

Abby cried out in fear. Somehow she managed to push Lance half off her and wriggle out from underneath him. She stood gazing down at him, her hands to her mouth, petrified, sure that she'd killed him. But after only a minute or so he groaned and began to stir. Then the full realisation of what he would do to her when he came round

hit her and fear brought movement to her frozen
limbs. She ran for the door just as he began to sit
up.

Her bag was still by the main door where
she'd left it, but she ignored it, instead picking
up Lance's car keys which were on the table
nearby. Behind her, she heard him call her name
and fear lent her wings as she rushed out into
the corridor. Not daring to wait for the lift, she
flew down the stairs, pulling her shirt together as
she ran. There were several people in the lobby
and they looked on in amazement as she tore
through them. There wasn't time to stop and
explain, to ask for help; she had to get away, as
far and as fast as she could. She erupted out of
the building and ran to where Lance's cars were
usually parked, but there was only the sports car
there. Of course, he wouldn't have left the Rolls
around in case she'd seen it and suspected that
he hadn't gone to Edinburgh. The door key was
obvious and she soon had it open and jumped
inside the car, but she didn't know which of the
other two keys fitted the ignition and her fingers
fumbled stupidly in her haste. But then she had
it, the engine starting at once with a rich,
throaty roar. Abby slammed it into reverse and
shot backwards, the tyres screaming. As she did
so Lance ran out of the building, the blood from
his cut head splashing on to his white shirt. He
started to run towards her, shouting something,
but the porter came after him and caught his
arm, gesturing to his head and obviously wanting
to help him. And those few seconds gave Abby
the precious time she needed to find first gear
and send the powerful car roaring out of the car
park into the roadway. As she went, she had just

a fleeting glance of Lance pushing the porter away and running back into the building.

At first she just drove, her heart thumping too fast for her to do anything but just hold the wheel and go, get as far away from him as possible, but then all sorts of things began to drop into place. She was filled with a great sense of foreboding and knew that there was one place she just had to go to.

The traffic was beginning to thicken up as the commuters left for home, and Abby didn't notice the blue Jaguar that kept always a few cars behind her as she headed south out of London. As she got further out the roads cleared and she put her foot down, using the power of the big car though half afraid of it, but not much caring because it began to look as if nothing much was going to matter any more. She had to stop twice to ask the way and it was almost six before she pulled up outside the Cassell Clinic. As she ran inside the Matron happened to be walking across the hall to her office. She stopped and looked at Abby enquiringly. 'Can I help you?'

'Yes. I came here before a few weeks ago. With Mr Bradbury.'

'Oh, yes, I thought I recognised you.' The woman smiled. 'You're his daughter, aren't you?'

'I? No, he came to . . .'

But the Matron was going on. 'I remember he said he was afraid you might be experimenting with drugs and he wanted to show you what it could do to people. I hope it did put you off?'

Abby stared at her. 'Yes. I mean . . . The girl we saw—what was her name?'

'Helen. Helen Andrews.'

'Is she—still here?'

'Oh, yes. She'll be here for a very long time, I'm afraid.'

'Could I see her again. *Please!*' Abby looked at her entreatingly.

'Well, I hardly think . . .' But then the woman saw the desperation in Abby's face and, although hardly understanding it, relented. 'Very well, I'll get one of the nurses to take you up.'

Nothing had changed. The room and the girl were just the same, her eyes still as vacant and empty. Only Abby's life had changed; her whole world was lying in jagged raw-edged pieces around her feet.

The Matron was still in the hall when they came down. She said goodbye and added, 'Please thank your father for his donation to the home, won't you? It's been a great help.'

The heavy wooden door closed behind her and Abby walked slowly down the steps. The fresh air felt good after the antiseptic smell of the Clinic; the evening sun cast a golden glow over the surrounding gardens and it was very warm; it would be a perfect summer night. She hardly even looked at Lance when he came and took her firmly by the arm and put her into the passenger seat of the Jaguar.

Abby didn't try to speak, she just sat staring at the windscreen, too stunned by Bradbury's duplicity to even be afraid of what lay ahead. Lance glanced at her from time to time as he drove back towards London, sure of his way and driving fast. The cut on his head was no longer bleeding and he had wiped the blood from his face, but it still stained his shirt, a sickening and unnecessary reminder of what she'd done to him. When they got back to his flat he again took her arm, but she went with him unprotestingly, completely drained of emotion.

At the porter's desk he paused and handed over the keys to the Jaguar. 'I borrowed Mr Seaton's car. See that he gets the keys back, will you?'

The porter looked at them both with avid curiosity and started to say something, but stopped short when he saw the look on Lance's face.

He took her up in the lift, still holding firmly on to her arm, and half dragged her into the flat, kicking the door shut behind them. Then he turned to her, his face grimly triumphant. 'And now,' he said savagely, 'we have some unfinished business, you and I.'

His menacing face filled her gaze as he loomed over her, but her vision had begun to blur at the edges. Waves of blackness washed over her as she said, 'Lance. Oh, Lance, I'm sorry.'

'It's too damned late to be sorry.'

His hands reached out for her and she put her own up in a futile attempt to hold him off, but then the waves of darkness came flooding back and she fainted, pitching forward into his arms.

When she came to, she was lying on the bed. Her face felt wet and she couldn't understand why. Slowly she turned her head and saw Lance standing over her. He must have put water on her face to bring her round, unable to even wait until she came to naturally. Abby turned her face away from him, desperately trying not to let him see her cry. But he reached over and turned her head towards him, then swore under his breath. He took a few angry paces up and down the room, than sat down abruptly on the edge of the bed.

'You'd better tell me exactly how you got into

this. All of it. I shall want you to write it all down and sign it later, too.'

'There's no need.' Abby put a fluttering hand up to her eyes. 'I've already written it down.'

'What do you mean?' Lance demanded sharply.

Tiredly she said, 'It's in my bag, by the door. There's a parcel; I was going to leave it here for you so that you'd find it when you got back from Edinburgh.'

He looked at her suspiciously for a moment, then decided that she had no fight left in her and went and fetched the bag. He took out the two parcels, then tore open the one addressed to himself. The box containing the Sarah Bernhardt necklace fell open and he looked first at it, then at Abby in surprise. The parcel also contained the tortoiseshell box, her engagement ring and the cameo brooch that he had given her, along with a long letter. He picked the letter up and began to read. In it Abby had recounted everything that had happened from her first meeting with Charles Bradbury. And she had finished the letter by saying: 'What you did to Sarah Bradbury is unforgivable, but I can't let you go to prison. You have time now to get away, to get out of England before you're found out and everyone learns the truth about you. Go quickly.' Then followed two words, heavily crossed out, and her name.

Lance stared at the letter and read the last paragraph through again, then picked up the parcel addressed to Bradbury and tore that open too. Inside was the silver bracelet that Bradbury had instructed her to buy at the start of her masquerade, along with a cheque and a note. The note simply stated that Abby had done all that she promised and no longer wanted any part in the affair, that she had sold the clothes she had bought and was returning the money she had got for them along with all that he had already paid her.

'Why did you do this?' Lance demanded rather hoarsely. 'Why send the money back that he'd paid you?'

Abby sighed tiredly. 'What does it matter?'

'It matters,' he said, and something in his voice made her look at him quickly, her eyes widening. 'Tell me,' he insisted. 'Why did you give Bradbury his money back? Why couldn't you let me go to prison?'

She licked lips gone suddenly dry. 'You—you know why.'

'No. How can I know?' He took hold of her wrists, his grip hurting her. 'Tell me,' he commanded for the third time.

'Because—because I love you,' she whispered, then quickly turned her head away, realising that her pathetic admission would only be another weapon against her.

There was a long silence before Lance released her wrists and said harshly, 'You have a damned funny way of showing it.'

Turning to look at him, she saw that he had a hand to the cut on his head, his lips twisting into a painful grimace. Quickly she sat up. 'Oh God, Lance, I'm sorry. Is it very bad? Oughtn't you to have it stitched? I thought—I was afraid—that you were going to—to rape me.'

He looked at her sardonically. 'You're right—I was.' Then, suddenly, he was angry again. 'You crazy little idiot! Why didn't you tell me the truth? I gave you every opportunity to do so. Time and time again . . .' He broke off and got to his feet, stood glaring down at her. 'At first I almost believed you were genuine. You didn't throw yourself at me like the others had done, and then you were so nervous of me that day we went to Oxford. I began to hope . . . but then you gave me that pen with the bug in it and I knew that I'd been right to be suspicious,' he said bitterly. 'You were just acting the part of a rich bitch!'

Abruptly, he turned and strode away, out into the sitting-room. Abby followed more slowly, and stood in the doorway, afraid to go in.

Lance poured himself a stiff whisky, then turned to face her. 'Oh, you were clever—very clever. But even so you gave yourself away. When we first met you told me that you'd stayed in Italy with your aunt, but later, when we had dinner in that Italian restaurant, you said that you'd never been there. And that day when you'd said you went for a walk on Hampstead Heath; I'd had you followed and he took the photograph of you with Bradbury.' He pointed to the photos still lying on the table.

'You kissed me that day,' Abby said slowly. 'You said that the kiss was for you. You—you sounded strange.'

His jaw tightened and he took a long swallow of his drink. 'Maybe because I saw you for the first time as the girl you really were. And maybe because I wasn't playing a part right then either.' He turned his back, as if he couldn't bear to look at her. 'You weren't very clever that day. You let me wait up there while you changed and I saw the bugs in your handbag. So I made it easy for you to plant them; taking you to my office and here to my flat, making sure you were left alone so that you could put them in place. I wanted to be done with it; to expose you and Bradbury and have you finished and done with.' His voice was raw with remembered anger, but then it changed as he said unsteadily, 'After you'd planted the bugs in my office I phoned your flat, but you didn't answer. I thought you'd cleared out and I went round there. But you'd been crying. I hoped then that you'd tell me the truth, but you didn't.'

'That was the night you proposed to me,' Abby reminded him.

'Yes.' He swung round to face her again, his jaw set. 'I thought that Bradbury wouldn't be able to resist the opportunity of really hurting me through you, if he thought I was in love with you. And as my fiancée you would be in a position to find out everything he wanted to know.'

'So why do it then?' Abby demanded. 'Why didn't you just go to the police?'

He shrugged. 'The only definite proof I had was the photo of you with Bradbury. And why expose you when he might try some other way? Better the devil you know than the devil you don't,' he added in a tone that made her flinch. 'And I wanted both of you, not just you alone. You and your lover,' he said insultingly.

Her face chalk-white, Abby went back into the bedroom, picked up the things from Bradbury's parcel and stuffed them into her bag with clumsy fingers, then started for the front door.

'Just where the hell do you think you're going?' Lance demanded grimly, setting his glass down with a snap.

'I don't have to stay here and take any more insults from you. If you want me punished, then go to the police. I'm sure you'll be able to tell them where to find me. I know I deserve what's coming to me, but I'm not taking any more from you.'

'Why not? You enjoyed taking your pound of

flesh by making me tell you that I loved you,
didn't you?'

'But that wasn't true.'

'You thought it was.'

'Yes.' Abby began to shake. 'You hadn't said it.
And I wanted to hear you say it. To—to remember.'

'Dear God!' Lance cursed under his breath.
'Abby, look at me.'

She obeyed, but her eyes were so misted with
tears she could hardly see him.

'I love you,' he said gratingly. 'And, God help
me, I can't live without you.'

Abby stared at him, hardly believing her ears,
but then he started towards her and she dropped
her bag and ran into his arms, clinging to him as if
she was afraid he might disappear at any minute.
Lance's arms went round her and he held her
close, his face buried in her hair. 'Why didn't you
tell me?' he groaned hoarsely. 'Why didn't you tell
me the truth?'

'I wanted to. But I was afraid?'

'Of me?'

'Yes,' she confessed. 'Because of what I thought
you'd done. He cheated me, Lance. They told me
at the Clinic. You were right; he never had a
daughter. It was someone else.'

'You soft-hearted little fool! Of course it was.
Didn't it once occur to you that if Bradbury could
use you to trick me, why couldn't he trick you into
doing what he wanted as well?'

'No.' She shook her head. 'But now I think he
even bribed my agent into refusing jobs for me, so
that I'd work for him. And I was so unhappy. You
seemed so different from what he'd said. I loved
you so much, and yet I thought you were cruel and
ruthless.'

'And I loved you and I *knew* you were a cheat. I think that's what made me so angry today, because I loved you so. But then you took my car and I could see it all happening again; you being killed. God, I was never so afraid in my life! If I'd lost you ... If I needed anything to make me realise how I felt it was that.'

'Oh, Lance!' Her fingers went up to gently touch the cut on his head. 'I'm sorry. I'm so sorry.'

'Don't ever say that again.' he told her roughly. 'It's over. Finished. And at least we found each other.'

'Then—kiss me. Won't you, please?'

Lance grinned at her crookedly. 'Any time, ma'am!'

It was a long time before either of them had time for words. They kissed like two people who had been apart for years, each hungry in their passion, wanting to give and to take at the same time, neither of them holding any thing back.

When at last they parted Abby sighed contentedly. 'That was for me—the real me.'

Lance sat down in the armchair and pulled her on to his knee, his arms round her possessively. 'You know, I'd begun to suspect that you cared some time ago, but I think I knew you were really in love with me when I saw the way you reacted to that photo of the girl I was engaged to. You weren't acting then, that was for real.'

Abby looked at him, a question in her green eyes.

'And what I said then still holds good; I got over her death a long time ago. And there hasn't been anyone I've been at all serious about since.'

'But plenty of other women,' Abby remarked only half teasingly.

He grinned. 'Of course—I'm far from being a monk! Anyway, what about you? I suffered agonies of jealousy when you were in your flat with Ross Newton.'

Abby stared at him. 'Even then?'

'Yes,' he admitted ruefully, 'even then. I wanted you like hell from the first moment I saw you.'

'Oh, Lance!' Abby started to say she was sorry again, but he put a finger on her lips. She smiled and changed it to a soft, 'I'll make it up to you, my darling.'

'You never called me that before.'

'I couldn't. Not then. But I wanted to so much.'

'Idiot,' he said, kissing her lingeringly. Then, some time later, 'Abby, you know you said you wanted to make it up to me . . .?'

She laughed. 'Don't you want to start again, make a new beginning?'

'No, I don't,' he told her forcefully. 'It's the ending I'm interested in.'

Abby smiled down at him, her eyes, her face, full of love and tenderness. 'Then let's make it a happy one, my darling.'

'It will be,' he assured her softly. 'For ever after.'

Harlequin Plus

A WORD ABOUT THE AUTHOR

Sally Wentworth began her career in the world of publishing by landing a newspaper job in the busy Fleet Street district of London, England. She thoroughly enjoyed the hectic atmosphere and the feeling that she was part of an organization determined to be the first with news and tops in circulation.

When she married, she left London and moved with her husband back to the rural county of Hertfordshire, just north of London, where she had been raised. Here she worked for the publisher of a group of magazines.

But the day came when her own writing made its claim on her energy and time. She began evening classes in creative writing and wrote free-lance articles for a number of magazines. One more step brought her to full-length book writing: her husband took on some evening work and she used the hours alone to write her first Harlequin—*Island Masquerade* (Romance #2155), published in 1978.

There have been a good many Sally Wentworth books since that first one—happily for her readers, who may not realize that Sally writes each manuscript by hand, being a much faster thinker than a typist!

Enter a uniquely exciting new world with

Harlequin American Romance ™.

Harlequin American Romances are the first romances to explore today's love relationships. These compelling novels reach into the hearts and minds of women across America... probing the most intimate moments of romance, love and desire.

You'll follow romantic heroines and irresistible men as they boldly face confusing choices. Career first, love later? Love without marriage? Long-distance relationships? All the experiences that make love real are captured in the tender, loving pages of **Harlequin American Romances.**

What makes American women so different when it comes to love? Find out with **Harlequin American Romance!**

Send for your introductory FREE book now!

Get this book FREE!

Harlequin American Romance

Twice in a Lifetime
REBECCA FLANDERS

Mail to:

Harlequin Reader Service

In the U.S.
2504 West Southern Avenue
Tempe, AZ 85282

In Canada
649 Ontario Street
Stratford, Ontario N5A 6W2

YES! I want to be one of the first to discover **Harlequin American Romance.** Send me FREE and without obligation *Twice in a Lifetime.* If you do not hear from me after I have examined my FREE book, please send me the 4 new **Harlequin American Romances** each month as soon as they come off the presses. I understand that I will be billed only $2.25 for each book (total $9.00). There are no shipping or handling charges. There is no minimum number of books that I have to purchase. In fact, I may cancel this arrangement at any time. *Twice in a Lifetime* is mine to keep as a FREE gift, even if I do not buy any additional books. 154 BPA NASD

Name _____ (please print)

Address _____ Apt. no.

City _____ State/Prov. _____ Zip/Postal Code

Signature (If under 18, parent or guardian must sign.)

This offer is limited to one order per household and not valid to current Harlequin American Romance subscribers. We reserve the right to exercise discretion in granting membership. If price changes are necessary, you will be notified.
Offer expires September 28, 1984

AR-SUB-200

Begin a long love affair with
SUPERROMANCE.
Accept LOVE BEYOND DESIRE **FREE.**

Complete and mail the coupon below today!

- -

FREE! Mail to: SUPERROMANCE